South-Facing House
and Other Stories

South-Facing House and Other Stories

Jagadish Mohanty

Translated from Odia by
Karunakar Mohapatra
Dr. Sachidananda Mohanty
Dr. Lipipuspa Nayak
Kamalakanta Mohapatra
Mitra Das

Edited by
Paul McKenna

BLACK EAGLE BOOKS
2019

 BLACK EAGLE BOOKS

7464 Wisdom Ln,
Dublin, OH 43016, USA
E-mail: info@blackeaglebooks.org
Website: www.blackeaglebooks.org

First International Edition published by
Black Eagle Books, 2019

South-Facing House and Other Stories by Jagadish Mohanty

Copyright of Original Odia © **Sarojini Sahoo**

English translation by individual translators
to Copyright of English translation © individual translators

Covern & Interior Design: Ezy's Publication

Library of Congress Control Number: 2019944375
ISBN- 978-1-64560-020-6 (Paperback)

Printed in United States of America

To our children
Anubhav & Sambedana

A FEW WORDS

With a heavy heart, I want to say a few words about the author of these stories. Jagadish Mohanty (17th February 1951-29th December 2013) was a renowned Odia writer considered as a trendsetter in modern Odia fiction, has received the prestigious Sarala award in 2003, Odisha Sahitya Akademi award in 1990. He was born in Gorumahisani iron mines area, Odisha. As his wife, it is my responsibility to make his stories reach more and more readers.

All stories in this collection were written between 1970 and 80. The title story South-Facing House was published in 1976 in a journal and gained huge readership and popularity. Most of his stories were experimental and philosophical. The language of his stories was poetic and lucid.

The author is no more. After his death, the late Karunakar Mohapatra, one of his admirer and retired professor in English, asked me to translate his stories in to English. Unfortunately, Professor Karunakar Mohapatra also left this world before completing the project.

I am thankful to **Dr. Sachidananda Mohanty** for translating *The Golden Fish*, **Dr. Lipipuspa Nayak** for translating *Rats*, **Kamalakanta Mohapatra** for translating *Sita in Ashok Forest* and **Mitra Das** for translating All Glitters.

- **Sarojini Sahoo**

CONTENTS

ALBUM

Age weighed heavily upon him. He was slightly bent at the waist. Specs on the eyes. Veins on the forehead, clearly visible. Bald head. He was sitting in a chair. There was a wall on the back. A calendar hung on the wall, a portion of which was captured in the photograph. That was the photo of my father. Underneath was written, "Srijukta Nagendranath Mohanty." I added 'late' to that name.

In the room the bed was as before. A red sheet was spread upon it. A quilt was at the foot but not used. There was a depression on the pillow; a clear mark of his head was still there. He was taken away as he was. He left the bed without a murmur of protest.

For a few days, he was suffering from fever. The doctor was sent for. After examining him, the doctor said it was typhoid and prescribed some capsules. The fever subsided. He took his bath and ate his usual meal of rice. At about three o'clock, he went around the village. He met the confectioner Madhu Sahu and told him since mango was plentiful this year, paddy crops would be good as well. He returned by four o'clock and told mother he had not urinated throughout the day and saying this, he went to urinate but could not. Slowly the discomfort increased.

The doctor was again called for. He came and put in a catheter and made him urinate. By then it was five o'clock. His condition had worsened. The doctor advised to take him to the district headquarters hospital at Baripada. If they did not succeed, then he would have to be shifted to SCB Medical College and Hospital at Cuttack. His guess was his kidney was not functioning properly.

Mother was nervous yet she had a reserve of strength. She did not break down easily. My cousins rushed to the Khunta bus stand to get a taxi. But as no taxi was available there, they had to go to Baripada and hire a taxi from there. By the time they reached the village, it was nine in the evening. Father was unconscious. He was talking incoherently. He was lifted physically from the bed and put into the taxi. Mother and two of my cousins accompanied him to Baripada. He was admitted to hospital there. He was punctured near the waist and some water was extracted for testing. Again, a catheter was used to make him urinate. Then he felt a little relieved and slept. He woke up at about four in the morning. My cousin asked him if he would take a sip of milk.

Father's eyes were shut. His voice came, as if, from far off. He said, "Have you brought? Then give me some."

My cousin helped him drink some milk. After drinking only half a glass, father began to doze. My cousin said, "Badapapa, some milk is still left." Father replied, "Left? All right, help me drink."

After drinking, he went to sleep quietly. Suddenly he called out the name of 'Tapan,' our servant boy who was very obedient to him. My cousin said, "Tapan is not here. You are in hospital."

Father said, "bring my sandals."

My cousin asked, "What are you going to do with sandals?"

Father sat up with a sudden jerk. When my cousin held him down tightly, Father said, "You don't understand. I have to go."

My cousin made him sleep and said, "No, you don't have to go anywhere. Just sleep here."

Father said feebly in a tone of defeat, "Well I am going. Put out the light." After saying this, all the milk he had taken came out through his nose.

His eyes were already shut. His lips trembled twice and then the end – he left for good. My cousin desperately called out "Barapada." Mother fainted.

I was not there with him. I was wandering about in Rourkela without any concern. A telegram was sent to me and when it arrived, I was at a movie theater. My neighbor had received it. The telegram was straightforward: "Father seriously ill. Come soon."

The next day at about eleven, I reached Baripada. At the bus stand, I met my cousin's brother Nunu and asked him about father.

Nunu Bhai could not speak for a few moments. His legs were trembling – I saw it clearly. After much hesitation he said, "Father is no more. He passed the night before yesterday. . . ."

I helplessly leaned against the tin body of the private bus which went from Baripada to Balasore via Udala. There was a darkness, like that when you are in a mine, which seemed to block my experiences. 'Til today, my acquaintance with death had only been through the obituary column in newspapers. For the first time in my life, I was told of the death of someone very near to me. My father had brought me to this world and had brought me up with much care. I wouldn't see him ever again. Before his name, the word 'late' would be added. I asked, who lit the pyre and heard that another cousin, Avinna Bhai, had done that.

We were five brothers and three sisters but none of us were present when the end came. The youngest, Devdutta, studied at Baripada. But he too was away with an excursion party. After his death, all the sons were informed by telegram: "Father seriously ill. Come soon." The daughters were not informed.

After receiving the telegram, besides me, those who arrived first were our eldest brother and our brother just above me – Somu Bhaina; Somdutta Mohanty was working as an engineer at Jajpur road. He had married just three months before and at that time, he had come home with his wife for the first time. My eldest brother had also come with his wife and children.

Their group photo was in my album. Besides them, others in the group were Somu Bhaina and Meena Apa. The photograph was a few years old now. At that time, my eldest brother was not very bald nor was his wife so very unattractive. Somu Bhaina was in shorts and a shirt, standing there with his hands crossed over his chest. Then, he was studying in school. Meena Apa, who was in class eight, was in a skirt and blouse. Beneath the photograph I had written, "flouring water."

What else was it but water flouring down? Time flew on or it got lost somewhere along the way. How could some people imprisoned in a half-cabinet-size photograph be expected to remain tied to each other forever? Somu Bhaina and Meena Apa were staying with our eldest brother at Bhubaneswar and studying there. Just as Somu Bhaina could not stay in his shorts and shirt forever, Meena Apa too had to discard her skirt and blouse and change into sarees. Both of them withdrew from that half-cabinet-size photograph. My eldest brother doubled his family size from two to four and built up their nest with a happy family. The owner of this happy family surrounded by a wall of happiness, our eldest brother, had come with a tape recorder, intending to tape father's voice.

He could not imagine father would have passed before he

left his voice on the tape. The tape recorder had been purchased sometime back, but eldest brother had not had the time to come and record his voice on the tape before now. By the time he could come, time had already waved its green signal.

I have not seen the tape recorder; it was in their box. Nobody talked about it. I only knew it had been brought from the conversation of eldest brother's wife.

As soon as I reached home, I could see the shadow of sorrowful tears all around. Seeing me, my eldest brother said, "Sidhi, father is no more." His voice trembled.

Mother hugged me in a tight embrace and said, crying, "I could not bring back your father. I am defeated." Saying this she cried and fainted. My eldest sister-in-law came out and seeing mother unconscious, she too cried and rolled on the ground. Somu Bhaina was trying to revive mother by sprinkling a little water on her face and eldest brother was consoling his wife.

Father was no more among us. This I realized. I realized too there was no more need to bend down and touch his feet, as I used to do every time I came home. There was nobody anymore to walk with me some distance to see me off when I went back the larger town where I worked. All of a sudden, I felt a vacuum inside me. A very real and very ruthless event had occurred. Before this reality, everybody seemed helpless. Tears came to my eyes.

Imprisoned in a half-cabinet-size photograph, Meena Apa, in a frock and two pigtails, was now a full-fledged housewife. Her husband was an engineer in the lift irrigation department at Karanjia. They had one son. Meena Apa was pregnant again and was near full-term. So how could such bad news be delivered to her at this critical moment? How could she come to the funeral ceremony? Would the long bus ride cause a problem for her? Lina Apa, too, was alone at Balasore. She was a lecturer there at the women's college. Would she not break down when the news reached her through letter or telegram? She was alone there. Who would console her? After long and intense discussion among all of us brothers, it was decided Nunu Bhai and I would go to Meena Apa and Lina Apa and tell them the sad news.

Nunu Bhai went to Balasore to break the news to Lina Apa, console her the best he could, and bring her home. My task was to inform Meena Apa after consulting her husband. If there were difficulties, I would have to give her the best consolation I could and come back home alone.

We started at ten o'clock. Bare feet, dress somewhat dirty. On the way, Nunu Bhai said to me, "Pick up a piece of straw, Sidhi." We can put the straw on the seat in the bus and sit on it. Nowadays, we cannot be sticklers for rules.

I could not accept it and said, "No, Nunu Bhai. Let it be. I can cover the distance by standing if will only take about 4-6 hours.

At the bus stand at Khunta, we found Manu Bhaina sitting with his wife. This was our sister-in-law's first visit to our place after leaving our village ten years ago on the plea of visiting her ailing grandfather. Her parental house was near the dwarfish Jagannath temple in Baripada. I was a high school student at the time at Khunta High School. I had come to help her get on the bus. She was a girl from Baripada. She could have gone alone. And she indeed went alone and never returned to our house during the last ten years.

I came to the bus stand to help her get on the bus. I was a fifteen-year-old school student in shorts at the time. Meanwhile, time had passed swiftly. Our sister-in-law had returned to our village which she vowed never to do when she left our house in a huff those many years ago. At that time, she was alone. Now she was accompanied by her husband Manu Bhaina and her two sons and a daughter. That day, I had come to Khunta bus stop. Today, too, I had come. That day, I came in shorts with school books in hand. Today, I came in bell-bottom trousers.

Khunta is our village bus stop; everybody knew us there. That was why sister-in-law covered her head with the end of her saree.

Ten years ago, when I came to see her off, I remember she had covered her head while coming to the bus stop. But as soon as she got on the bus, she removed the saree from her head, again became a girl, and said to me, "I can go alone, Sidhi. You may now go home."

Brother, seeing us, became a little flustered and asked us, "How is father?"

How could we answer? What could we say? How to express such a cruel reality? My throat was constricted. Nunu Bhai's voice too trembled, when he said, "The day the telegram was sent to you, that very morning, he passed."

Sister-in-law thumped down on the ground. Manu Bhai's legs began to shake. I could not look him in the eye; tears came to my eyes. While wiping away the tears with the back of my palm, I saw sister-in-law trying to admonish her children running here and there. She took the three-year-old boy and told them, "Don't be naughty. Your grandpa is no more."

The little boy seeing tears in his mother's eyes was puzzled and asked uncomprehendingly "Mama, why are you crying? What is our grandpa to you?"

A little boy barely three years old asking what our grandpa had to do with his mother. What could Manu Bhaina or sister-in-law say in reply? This question of a simple and innocent child; what a knife-like edge it had. As if the child was asking, Now tell me, what is Nagendra Mohanty to you? He gave you birth, fed you, took care of you, educated you, made you grow from childhood to manhood, helped you set up your family. What have you done for him? Tell me, what duties you have performed towards him?

I told them quietly, "Take off your sandals." And both of them removed their sandals.

We got onto the bus, Numu Bhai and me. We would travel together up to Baripada. From there, he would go to Balasore and I would go to Karanjia. Nunu Bhai could have gone to Balesore via Udala. But somehow, he wanted to go via Baripada. Maybe he felt uncomfortable to stand there at Khunta bus stop with Manu Bhai, or maybe he had some work at Baripada.

After getting onto the bus, I was lost in thought. A three-year-old child was asking what was my grandpa to you? And confronted with such a simple question, we had nothing to answer. The question followed me everywhere and to avoid it, I plunged deeper into the past. In my wanderings in the past, I stopped at a photograph in the album. It was the photo of a sixteen-year-old boy in shorts and banyan standing in the courtyard with hands crossed on his chest. That was Manu Bhaina's photo. I had written underneath, "Manu Mohanty, a star." Just beside it, there in another photo of Manu Bhai, was as a bridegroom. He was taking the ceremonial leave of mother before proceeding to the bride's house. He was wearing a dhoti and Punjabi with a tiara made of cork on his head and waiting for mother to give him 'Kanakanjali.' I remember clearly how Manu Bhaina had stood below the veranda under the eaves to receive mother's blessings. Mother was in the process of giving her blessings and permission and had cried. I was puzzled to see mother crying on such a happy occasion as her son's marriage. Much later, I understood that was the most heart-wrenching time for mothers. They relinquish all their claims and all their ties, and hand over their sons to another woman. I still saw the tears in mother's eyes whenever I looked at that photo. Underneath that photo, I wrote again, "the star that became a meteor."

Yes, what else but a meteor? That boy who was made of pure gold, who never answered back to his parents, never disobedient, always did well in his studies, whose parents had many dreams while sending him to engineering college, who loved his brothers and sisters more than his life. That boy, after getting married and living with his wife, forgot everything: father, mother, brothers and sisters, and his sense of duty. Why did this happen?

Who was to blame? Probably our Indian social mores. There was so much pretension in our system of values. Here, terms like 'character' and 'sense of duty' had become so very stale and yet we believed in them. On the other hand, selfishness had engulfed us. Self- interest had driven us apart. Even being related by blood could not keep us together yet we could not speak of it openly. We kept it all under wraps behind a false mask of filial and brotherly affections. But how long could this go on? In the tug of war between self-interest and this false and empty sense of values, it was selfishness which always won. And when it happened, there was an explosion which would shatter this false mask of pretention. Such good and obedient people like Manu Bhaina had turned into strangers and intentionally broke away from their family to build their own nest of happiness.

Manu Bhaina, have you become happy? Remember, you used to write poetry in your college days. You were in love with a Bengali girl who came from Betanati by bus to read in your college at Baripada. I came to know of it from the manuscript of your poems. No one in the family knew of it, nor did you recall it to anybody. Such affairs happened in life. Who holds unto them?

In a moment of tiredness, have you never opened the window of your past and felt helpless? School life at Khunta; College life at Baripada; a few lines from your old poems; that Bengali girl coming from Betanati to Baripada by bus; our house in Gayalmara. All these, have they never troubled you? Have you never felt the life you left behind was beautiful? Have you never felt a stirring in yourself to go back to that life?

Are you still happy? The white discharge of sister-in-law was increasing. You were tired of taking her to doctors. Doctors had said this disease would never be cured. You were apprehensive of it developing into cancer in the future. Sister-in-law was losing weight. Are you still happy? What is that happiness for which you abandoned your past; disregarded all the claims of blood; and went your way? You wanted liberation, Bhaina? Have you got it? Is there happiness in that freedom?

Thinking of all these things in a feat of forgetfulness, I had sat down on the seat. Recovering from my wandering thoughts, I suddenly became conscious of my transgression and stood up and looked through the window to see how far away Baripada still was.

When I got off the bus at Karanjia, I had no idea how to break this sad news to Meena Apa. I wandered around for some time; smoked a cigarette or two; drank a cup of tea standing before the tea stall; and decided to go to my brother-in-law's office and tell him the news and together decide what to do.

So I went to Lift Irrigation Office where my brother-in-law worked. The peon there told me Dibyendu Bhaina was there in the office. I entered through the screened door. He was surprised to see me and greeted me, "Oh poet, to what do I owe this sudden visit?"

I tried to smile but could not. I went forward to his table. He asked me to sit down but I said, "No, I can't sit down."

He was puzzled. Asked, "Why? What is it? What is the matter with you?"

This time I replied straight, "Father has passed."

He froze for a second and could not utter a word. Then he got up, came towards me and putting his hand on my shoulder, he asked, "When did this happen? How did it happen? Have you informed Meena?"

Under the pressure of his consoling hand, my shoulder was as if it was melting away in sorrow. I held on to the table. My feet were quivering. I said, "No, I have not yet gone to your house. She is in an advanced stage of pregnancy. I do not know if it would be right to tell her."

He thought for a moment, and then patting me on the back said, "Let us go home." He almost dragged me out of the office. On the way he said, "Sidhi, don't say anything to Meena. She may be too shocked at the news. Besides, she may insist on going to your village. At this stage, the journey by bus is risky. Her last delivery was by caesarean section and the stitches are still weak."

I was walking behind him looking at the ground. I was not in a state to think of anything. When we reached his quarters, I held back. When he was pressing the calling bell, I stood leaning against the wall away from the door.

Meena opened the door and asked him why he was home so early.

Dibyendu Bhaina replied with a laugh, "Sidhi has come."

So, I had to come forward. I did and touched Meena Apa's feet. I then remembered I had not greeted brother-in-law. But after talking to him for so long, I thought it wouldn't be right to greet him now, so I didn't.

Meena Apa said "Why are you so downcast? Look at the state of your shirt and trousers. Don't you feel ashamed to wander about dressed like this?"

I kept quiet. I even tried to appear bashful. Meena Apa saw my bare feet and asked, "What is the matter? Where are your sandals?" What could I say? Bhaina saved me by saying "Don't you know your brother is a little touched in the head? He lost his sandals on the way."

Meena Apa smiled. "Even the sandals vanish from your feet! You are as before, still a child," she scolded him. "When will you grow up? I'm afraid this business of writing poetry has turned your head around."

Meena Apa went inside smiling. She still did not know about father's death. I stayed behind in the drawing room. Brother-in-law followed Meena Apa inside. I not only stayed back. I went back farther and farther into the past, 'til I reached the quarter-cabinet-size photograph in the album. A girl of fourteen with two pig tails was standing beside a table full of cups and saucers. Underneath was written, "her face looks hazy."

That fourteen-year-old girl was lost somewhere. She used to demand six paisa from father every day after returning from her music lesson.

That girl was lost and now was only in the album. Beside it, there was another face, that of a 28-year-old woman, a mother who was cuddling a baby and looking at the camera. This photo too was of Meena Apa. The two photos in the album were separated only by an inch. Yet to cover this one-inch distance, she had to wait for 13 or 14 years. During this period, she had accumulated so many incidents, so many memories, and so many experiences.

Meena Apa, while studying at MPC College in Baripada fell in love with Dibyendu Bhaina. He went away to Burla to study engineering but they kept in touch. By the time Dibyendu Bhaina completed his engineering courses, Meena Apa had left college and was sitting at home. One day Meena Apa openly declared she would marry only Dibyendu and no one else. He was, of course, a very eligible groom and an engineer.

But our family was in a fix: Lina Apa, the elder sister of Meena Apa, was still unmarried. How could the younger sister get married before the older one? Lina Apa, by that time, was already a lecturer. She was on the verge of crossing marriageable age. Besides, she was an introvert, obstinate, dark-complexioned, serious, and without an eye for fashion. She was incapable of choosing a partner for herself. On the other hand, father was old and retired, somewhat negligent, idle, and indifferent. The brothers were busy with their own families. So then who would look for a groom for Lina Apa?

Meena Apa sought Lina Apa's help and she did help. In spite of father's and brothers' deep dissatisfaction, she made them all agree and Meena Apa's marriage took place. That same Meena Apa, who was studying at Baripada; who used to wait eagerly for Dibyendu's letters at our home in Gayalmara; who, at night, used to read this letters hidden in the folds of book; who used to stand before the mirror and covering her head with the end of her saree, who used to feel a little shy; and today, that same Meena Apa, a mother of a child and soon, to be a mother of another child. What a difference! Such a great gulf was between the past and the present. Was this gulf life?

I was in the drawing room. Meena Apa called me loudly from the inside, "Sidhi, why don't you come inside? Where did you come from? Did you go home? How are the parents?"

No words came out. Dibyendu Bhaina changed the topic and asked me, "Now poet, what are you writing now?"

This was a peculiarity of Dibyendu Bhaina. Whenever we met, he always asked me about poetry. It didn't mean he was a lover of modern poetry. It seemed he did not have any other subject about which to talk with me.

Meena Apa asked if I would stay for three or four days.

I said, "No, I will go away within the hour."

Meena Apa then got angry. She scolded, "Then why did you come? Every time you come, you just go away after showing your face. None of you are visiting me. Why? Devadutta is at Baripada. It is not a very distant place from Karanjia."

I replied "Listen Meena Apa. I promise next time I shall surely stay with you for three or four days. And you have to sing for me – a lot of songs."

Meena Apa became silent. She became probably absent-minded as well. After a while she said, "I don't know, Sidhi. I haven't sung for a long time now. I may have forgotten what I used to sing." She fell silent again. Then she said, "Come, take your bath now. I'm going to set the table."

After lunch, when I started to leave, Meena Apa tried to stop me but Divyendu Bhaina said "He probably has some work to do. See his condition: several days' growth of beard, soiled clothes, no luggage. Let him go to Baripada now."

Meena Apa did not insist. When I touched her feet, she said, "Take care of yourself. You're doing a lot of running around in the sun, na? You have become as dark as a piece of charcoal. Why are not you shaving? Try to be neat and clean. See that you don't lose your sandals again."

Divyendu Bhaina came to see me off at the bus stop. It was terribly hot that day. Even the tar on the road was melting; it was painful to walk in bare feet. So I walked on the earthen fringe of the road instead. We both were silent, swimming in a sea of silence, unable to find words. Yet both of us were thinking about the same thing – father's death. News of death often makes one silent, at least for some time.

I asked him at the bus stop, "How will you break this news

to Meena Apa?" He fell silent and then after a while, said, "Let us see how the situation develops."

Again, we were both silent. Someone on the road greeted Divyendu Bhaina. We were silent. A rickshaw passed us by ringing his bell. We were silent. A Marwari gentleman asked, in broken Odia, about Divyendu Bhaina's wellbeing. He simply nodded his head. We were silent.

After a lengthy silence, Divyendu Bhaina said, "Explain our situation to everybody at home. I may attend the tenth-day ceremony but I have some problems here. Meena is almost full term now and the first delivery was done by caesarean section.

He was silent; I was silent. There was silence all around. In this all-encompassing silence, dead words of the crowd, of their quarrel, of buses, rickshaws, of trees and leaves of sands – all are meaningless. Suddenly Divyendu Bhaina said, "Here is your bus."

I bent down and touched his feet. When I arrived, I forgot to wave my hand to him. He patted me on the shoulder and said, "Okay, Okay. Enough."

When I arrived, all except Meena Apa had come home. In the beginning, when someone came from the bus and reached home, there was a lot of crying. That cry come from the depth of the heart and made all our hearts melt and dragged us to tears as well. Every time this happened, I used to run away from home. I knew mother would faint after a bout of crying. Water would be sprinkled on her face to revive her and then a detailed recital of death would be repeated.

I did not have the courage to face all this. Death was such a thing before which all our values, our personality, and the strange and mysterious habit of clinging to life appeared meaningless. I was an ordinary man who wrote stories, loved, and drempt of a happy family who wanted some stability and broke down without it. I was so weak inside I could not get the strength to stand up firmly. How would I face such a tearful truth?

Avinna asked me, "Sidhi, what was troubling uncle? Was there a monetary problem? When we took him to the hospital, he was blubbering in the taxi about 12 rupees, 14 rupees, twenty rupees, only 46 rupees. 'Avinna, I do not have any more money. I have become poor.' Why was he talking like that?"

I became quiet. Some days back, father had written to me for money. I had replied then I would not be able to send any money then as I had just sent money to Devadutta. Father had, of course, written to all his sons for money. Somu Bhaina had sent only 50 rupees. As an explanation, he added that as he was going to set up home with his wife and the cost of establishment had gone up; he wouldn't be able to spare any money then and in the future. Manu Bhaina did not reply at all. The eldest brother wrote that as his wife's sister had come and she had to be given a costly saree and other things and the market being what it was, he was in no position then to send any money.

I knew mother's medicine cost 12 rupees, 20 rupees towards a radio license fee with a fine, and a further 14 rupees towards its repair. The balance of four rupees was spent on his capsules for typhoid. At this time in summer, the thatch on the roof had to be changed. Annual sowing of the paddy crop was ahead and for that, money would be required. So, there were a lot of expenses to be considered.

All the produce of the last crop was spent during Somu Bhaina's marriage. We were all living far away and remained unconcerned after sending a postcard stating our inability or unwillingness to send money. Now, father had to face all his problems alone.

Could I not have sent 50 rupees if I really tried? I always spent 50 to 60 rupees a month just on smoking. Also, I spent money in restaurants unnecessarily. Couldn't Somu Bhaina have sent 50 rupees every month after making some adjustments in his home budget? How could he say no to father's request for help? Eldest brother could have stopped buying cassettes for his tape recorder for some time or he could have saved some money by spending less on his wife's sister and helped father out. Manu Bhaina too could have . . .

Yet nobody could be blamed for this. Who could be blamed? We had drifted so much apart from each other and so very restricted by our own orbits, we were not capable of empathy for anyone's problems. Our desire for happiness and our effort to keep up our prestige had driven us apart. Who among us now remembered father, in his desire to bring us up well and to educate us had forgone all his little pleasures; had borrowed money on interest; had even economized on food and dreamed that once we were established in life, all his problems would be solved? To what extent did we fulfill his dreams?

Father was a clerk in TISCO at Gorumahishani. At that time, to educate us well, he sent us to schools and colleges outside and bore the expenses of putting us in hostels. He spent almost his entire salary on us. Still, he somehow managed his household necessities.

When eldest brother got a job, the Gorumahishani mines were closed down. Father came back home and spent his retirement money on building a two-room thatched house with a varanda all around.

We came from towns. We felt suffocated in the dark rooms in our old low-level thatched house. So our new house had a high roof with wide windows. All his money was spent on building this house. Yet the day the house was consecrated by proper puja and we made a formal entry into the house, father expressed his satisfaction and said that a long-standing dream of his had been fulfilled; one's own home was the happiest place to live in. When he said this, his eyes shone with happiness. But today, father left the house he had built himself with his own hands the safe haven he had created for himself. What was left behind were only memories and happiness, and the picture of his two shining eyes on the pages of my mind.

Father had a money-box. I had seen him once sitting with that box in the village. At that time, father depended eventually on eldest brother's help. Manu Bhaina too had a job and he bore the expenses of Somu Bhaina's and Lina Apa's education. Once I saw father in an evening open the box and count the money. There was actually no money in the box, only a few coins. How much was it? At most about two or three rupees. Yet he counted those coins again and again. That sight made me feel helpless. I knew the money brother sent was all spent the day it arrived. Now he had to manage the whole month with only those coins. Devadutta and I myself were staying in the village with parents. I was a student of Class nine or ten in Khunta High School and Devadutta was studying in the middle school of the village.

That scene still floats before my eyes and I still feel helpless. Father sitting there with the money box open before him and counting the few coins again and again. There was no more money in it. The worry shown all over his face. This scene floated before me and I felt sorrow in my heart. I felt I was worthless, incapable. Depending on me, on us, father was failing in his attempt to get into his dream train and we, all of us, were unable to help. Is it because of this father left us carrying his hurt and pride in his heart?

His hurt/pride was against everybody, we the sons, mother, and even Lina Apa. Father knew mother had about hundred rupees hidden somewhere. Mother had saved it for use in times of need. Father always used to pester mother for his money. It was a kind of pleasant family game. Mother had a number of small glass jars and old dry milk tins where she kept sugar, oil etc. During mother's absence father brought them out from the dark room. Mother would know of it and grumbled she had saved a little only to help in times of need and father had his eyes on that little money. Father flattered her and pleaded with her to help him out only this time and promised to pay her back next month when money came from their sons. This kind of hide and seek constantly went on between father and mother.

This time, father really needed money. None of the sons were ready to help. It was not a matter of one month only. The future too depended on it. Without money, how could he cultivate the land? Clear pay for food? Father was very anxious and asked mother for some money. She had money but she refused on the basis of it was for future needs. She said she had given the money to her daughter-in-law when they left home to settle in a distant town but father knew that mother was lying. He did not ask a second time. He remained glum sitting there for a long time and was heard complaining telling that the whole world was selfish. This was what mother heard.

Father's delirium had started right at Gayalmara. When cousins Nunu and Avinna went to call a taxi, father was talking incoherently lying on the bed. Mother was alone, terrified, and did not know what to do. Desperately, she brought out the 130 rupees she had saved and thrust it into father's hand. Even in that condition of incoherence, making that miserable calculation of 12 rupees, 20 rupees, and 14 rupees, he threw away the money and blubbered "I don't need any of this. All is a lie, illusion. I have become poor. I am finished. Everything I built up is shattered. Everything. My family, my home and heath. Everything."

Some of it I heard from Nunu Bhai and some from mother. I also heard that sometime back, when father was suffering from fever, a registered parcel from Lina Apa had arrived. Before that a post card had come. In it Lina Apa had written:

"Rajo festival is near. A lungi, a dhoti and a vest for you. A sambalpuri saree for mother and for Devadutta, trousers and shirts. I thought of going home with these but the door of our house was shut for me. What claim did I have to come home? Moreover, since I vowed never to go home, I will send all these by post. Hope you will be pleased.

Yours obediently

Lina"

Reading the letter father's eyes, at first, brimmed with tears. But later on, he became terribly angry and had said to the postman to return the packet. Mother, Nunu Bhai, and Avinna managed to pacify him and after signing the paper, he accepted it. The packet, however, was never opened. It was still lying there. Father, in his wounded pride, had said to mother, "Keep it away. Open it when

I am dead. Your daughter has sent a dhoti. It will be of use to you when you are a widow."

Mother had bullied father, "Why are you speaking of such inauspicious things at this time of evening?

Father was sitting leaning against the wall, tired, looking vacantly at the sky, eyes brimming with tears. There was a story behind his being wounded and brokenhearted. There was not much substance in the story but time and situation added substance to it. The story was something like this:

A few months back, during Somu Bhaina's marriage, a small quarrel erupted between Lina Apa and Somu Bhaina over something insignificant. Lina Apa was like that. It was difficult to understand her moods. She would make a mountain out of a mole hill. She was quite obstinate from her childhood. In our middle-class families, no attention was ever paid to the mental development of a child. All the little complexes which took shape in her childhood had become big and true and spread their roots all over later in her life.

There was a photo in my album. Plain-looking, without any attempt at fashion nobody could say she was a lecturer, although her eyes shone with the light of knowledge and her face was intelligent. But there were also hidden scars of many wounds and hot fumes of wrath in her bright face. That was a photo of an introvert girl and she was my Lina Apa. Below the photograph I had written, "smell of imaginary explosives."

She was always angry about males in general. She could not appreciate her brothers who, after marriage, gradually drifted apart and remained shut up selfishly in their own family life. She poured all her anger out on her father and her brothers, who became for her representatives of the male faction of humanity. Of course, I, Somubhaina, and Devadatta, as younger brothers, shared some of this anger. But the target of her most intense anger was father, though father loved her the most. The cause of her accumulated anger against father was her non-marriage and she held father mainly responsible for the lack of interest in arranging a marriage for her. Father was so helpless in the grip of this feeling of guilt that as a result, he loved Lina Apa a little more. But Lina Apa never could appreciate that love and affection. She got a kind of mental satisfaction out of hurting father.

During Somu Bhaina's marriage, father and Lina Apa were quarreling over something trivial. At this time, father passing by said to them, "There are a lot of things to be done. Why are you wasting time? Go and do some work." The remark father made was innocuous. Father did not know why they were quarreling, nor did he support anyone. Yet she made it a point of her argument. Her argument was: father didn't want her to come home. If she did come, she had to work like a maidservant; bear all insults silently – that's what father wanted - and she would have to remain a maid to her brothers throughout her life etc., etc.

All this anger, all her wounded feelings appeared childish to me. I often wondered how can a lecturer of history who was capable of thinking intellectually be so childishly quarrelsome and nurse her grudge of wounded feelings?

Father was haunted by such accusations. Still he did not take it to heart and tried to modify her; tried to remove her anger and her frustration. But Lina Apa, once she gets angry, however insignificant may be the cause of that anger, would nurse it for a long time and sometimes, all her life, she wouldn't forget it. That was why after so many years of Somu Bhaina's marriage, she sent that parcel to remind father she had not forgotten nor forgiven, and by reminding, to hurt him. Was that hurt a bit too much? Father, for the first time in his life, felt towards Lina Apa that feeling of wounded pride, which in the end, probably proved suicidal.

In the evening, there was an informal meeting. All the brothers, elder sister and her husband, Avinna, Nunu Bhai, Father's younger brother, and Lina Apa were present. Mother was the convener of the meeting. Devadatta had spread a mattress on the ground. All the male members sat on it. Mother, Lina Apa, and elder sister sat near the door sill. Avinna, with his lungi tucked up, sat on the ground. Just when the meeting was about to start, elder sister went inside to feed her daughter. Brothers' wives were all inside, only eldest brother's wife sometimes passed by to see and hear what was going on.

There were two subjects on the agenda: the care of mother in the future and the expenses to be incurred for father's funeral ceremony. On the first, everybody agreed that mother could not be left alone in the village and all the sons and Lina Apa expressed their willingness to take on the responsibility. Elder sister and her husband kept quiet as they had nothing to say about it.

The first topic was raised by father's younger brother and the matter was left to mother to decide with whom she would stay, and she was asked to make her decision known by the thirteenth day of the funeral ceremony. Everybody agreed that their farm land would be tenanted.

The second topic was raised by mother herself. For father's treatment, some money was taken on loan from Avinna and Nunu Bhai and it was the responsibility of the sons to repay that loan. All the expenses for funeral pyre were born by uncle, father's younger brother. That too was to be repaid. Other expenses for the after-death ceremony were to be met from the paddy and rice stock at home. But the main thing was from the seventh day after death, the ceremony would start. A budget should be prepared for the expenses involved, and from where the money would come, and who would contribute what amount should be made clear straight away. Another thing was Avinna had lit the funeral pyre. So by custom, he would have to observe all the rules involving death and on the ninth day, he would have to offer the customary sacred food to the departed spirit. It was a point to be decided by the Brahmin Pundit whether Avinna could transfer his responsibility to some other brother and if so, how.

The sum and substance of what uncle said was he had incurred the expenses of the funeral pyre as a duty of a younger brother towards his elder brother and he would not take any money for that from his nephews. Then, he said he knew from his experience 3,000 rupees would be needed for the whole funeral ceremony: 1,000 rupees for feeding all the clan members for three or four days; another thousand towards cost of buying clothes for everybody; and a further thousand towards feeding the Brahmin and the village people on the eleventh day. So altogether, 3,000 rupees would be sufficient to conclude the whole ceremony.

Uncle opined this expense should be shared by all the sons. Father had four sons and all of them were earning. So if the four sons contributed 750 rupees each, then all the expenses could be met without much difficulty. And about religious formalities, he said he would consult the family priest.

The first one to oppose this proposal was the eldest brother. He said it wouldn't be possible on his part to contribute 750 rupees. He said, after constructing a house at Budheswar colony in Bhubaneswar, he was under the pressure of a loan. Manu Bhaina, in his short speech, said it was not possible for him to contribute that sum either, as his financial condition was very bad. Somu Bhaina said he had recently set up a family and from where could he get that money.

So, the solution of this problem was evident from what they said. They were all of the opinion some land would have to be sold to meet the expenses. This proposal of the three brothers was vehemently opposed by mother and Lina Apa. The atmosphere at the family meeting became very tense as the three brothers were on one side and mother and Lina Apa were on the other side argued with each other. Eldest sister and her husband did not participate in this farce. All the daughters-in-law, hearing the commotion, came to the door and the eldest and second sister-in-law were heard whispering their husbands were right. The meeting broke up and uncle, very annoyed, left in a huff.

As Avinna and Nunu Bhai were not expected to say anything, they only enjoyed the farce and left. Even after the meeting broke up, the dying embers still remained, though the details of that are unnecessary.

An hour after this incident, mother and Lina Apa were sitting in the dark; someone had taken away the lantern. I went and sat down beside Lina Apa. I said "Lina Apa, I can arrange for 1,500 rupees. How much can you arrange? Can't you get a loan from your GPF (General Provident Fund - a government loan program)?"

Lina was thoughtful and said somewhat hopelessly she could but it wouldn't be possible within such a short a period of time to apply, get approval, and draw money. When I said I had talked to Avinna and he had agreed to lend 3,000 rupees on condition if we could not pay him back within three months, we would have to sell him that particular piece of fertile land he coveted. Lina Apa became silent for some time and then asked mother what she thought about it. Mother asked us both if we could really repay 1,500 rupees each within three months. We both told her yes, we could.

So it was agreed we would borrow money from Avinna and conduct father's funeral ceremony. Mother was a little relieved but tension continued within the family. All were silent, only whispering sometimes. If anyone else came along, they again fell silent and would look at him or her suspiciously. This was as if not a home but a chessboard. Here we all were gathered for father's death ceremony but instead were plotting how to make the best move with the pieces we had. In a corner of that chessboard mother, myself, and Lina Apa were sitting in the darkness under the open sky dumb, helpless, and alone.

The family priest said Avinna could not transfer his responsibility to anyone else until the ninth-day ceremony had been completed which meant Avinna had to observe all the customary rules.

The rules included sleeping on a bed of straw; go without shaving; wear nothing on the feet; and wear a single piece of dhoti for the entire period.

The three brothers and their wives occupied whatever space they could find. Ours was a double-roofed thatched house. One room contained paddy, rice, trunks, almirahs etc. In another room was goddess Laxmi's shrine and other things. There was a veranda around all the rooms. At one end of the veranda, a kitchen was constructed by partitioning a portion with a wall. In the front part, a drawing room was made. Behind it there was a storage room. The rest was grabbed by eldest brother, Manu Bhaina, and eldest brother-in-law; after that, there was almost no space left. During this period of mourning, nobody could sleep on cots. So, all the wooden cots and stringed ones were removed. The room containing the shrine of goddess Laxmi was occupied by Somu Bhaina. After all the senior members monopolized the bedding and pillows, only a mattress and one pillow were left. Lina Apa spread that mattress on a portion of the veranda. There, mother, Lina Apa, Devadatta, and I would sleep. I slept without the pillow leaving it for mother; mother left it for Lina Apa; and Lina Apa left it for Devadutta. In the middle of the night when I woke, I found Devadutta laying by my side and then mother and then Lina Apa. The pillow was nowhere near us.

None of us were in the habit of sleeping on the ground. Manu Bhaina first raised the objection by saying his children did not have the habit of sleeping on the ground. They would fall sick if they did. Mother said, "They are not sons; they are grandsons. So, they can sleep on cots."

But I was filled with sudden anger at Manu Bhai's words. I said, "You, Manu Bhaina, are so changed now; I had no idea. You have come to attend father's funeral ceremony and you are looking for a pretext to sleep on a cot in comfort."

Lina Apa was more forthcoming. "Have your children come to attend their grandfather's funeral or have they come to a marriage party to make merry? If you cannot sleep on the ground, then you should not have come."

Our words hurt Manu Bhaina and his wife. He stated Sidhi and Lina couldn't tolerate their children. And his wife, to drive the point further, said since Lina did not have the good fortune to be a mother, how could she know what children were like?

Lina Apa was so hurt by this she went on grumbling and

chiding for a long time. When eldest brother commented Lina Apa should not have bossed over an elder brother, another round of quarrel erupted. This disagreeable quarrel would have continued if uncle had not come and scolded everybody and reminded all of us we were gathered there for father's funeral and not for fighting with each other. Uncle's intervention probably would not have stopped this infighting if mother hadn't fainted after a bout of crying at such unnecessary behavior. So the quarrel subsided, but the tension remained, like the embers of a dying pyre.

In the garden behind our house under a mango tree, I was sitting on a mattress and looking at the photographs in my old album. I stopped at a photo of father. It was taken at Gorumahisani when he was in the service; bald-headed, thick moustache under a high nose, and the promises of self-sufficiency in his eyes. He was standing on the floor of the studio in his usual dhoti and Punjabi. Underneath the photo I had written "strong foundation."

This comment I had written when father was alive. In my childhood, father looked very big to me. Tall, healthy, but as I grew up, he somehow looked smaller and smaller. Yet I always melted before his personality. Except Lina Apa, we all melted before him. We would never have enough courage to answer him back. And now after his death, how could we forget him so soon? My comment "strong foundation," was it really that strong? Then how could the fibers and veins of a close-knit family snap so easily? Or maybe we were gradually losing our hearts? Were we losing our hearts? Were we losing our sensitivity?

Otherwise, how could we all be forgetting such a great emptiness in our lives, fight for our self-interest and our ego? Manu Bhaina once suffered from pneumonia. At that time, mother was pregnant with Lina Apa. I had heard during that time, father would cook for the family, work during the day, and after work, would hold Manu Bhaina on his lap the whole night. Currently, Manu Bhai wouldn't sleep on the ground during father's funeral ceremony and was more worried about his children falling ill.

Camu's "Outsider" came to mind. The protagonist of that story had no feeling of sorrow after his mother's death. I used to often think Camu was probably exaggerating for who didn't cry at one's mother's death? But what could I say today? How little was the difference between the hero of "Outsider" and eldest brothers Manu Bhaina and Sonu Bhaina? And what about me? Was I really in the grip of real sorrow? Had I really cried my heart out? Had I too lost my sensitivity as well? There was a little emptiness in my heart but where was the real feeling of sorrow?

Man was forever man. Beyond all geographical, social and cultural boundaries, all men were the same. All were more or less outsiders. It was a strange game for the creator and controller of this world. Man clung to life knowing full well that life was meaningless. Today he was alive; tomorrow he may die. No one would remember you after death. You would remain forgotten on a page in an album for some time. That's all. Why then was man so enmeshed in the web of selfishness, jealousy, and violence? Why set up a family at all then? Why brag about my wife, my son, my daughter? Tell me, who was my own in this world?

The whole day I remained drowned in thought. A kind of helplessness had me in its grip. The meaninglessness of life enveloped me completely. I felt I should leave this world and become a sannyasi. What was the use of being caught in such an illusion? Who was my own? Everybody was after self-interest, after money. Father, to bring up his children, sacrificed everything: his life, his earnings, his happiness. Now his sons are unwilling to spend a few hundred rupees for his funeral ceremony.

For eldest brother, building a house in Buddheswari colony was more important than father's funeral; for Sonu Bhaina, setting up a home was more important, and for Manu Bhaina, the smile on his wife's face was more important than father. What did father gain?

The whole day I remained in a grave mood. I was doing everything but in a state of absent mindedness. That single thought kept going around in my head. In the evening, I was sitting alone in the darkness; up above in the sky, stars had come out. It was a dark night as the moon had not risen yet. Lina Apa came and asked me, "Sidhi, what are you thinking of sitting all alone in the dark?"

I did not reply. Putting her palm on my head she continued, "Are you grieving? What's the use of grieving? Will father come back? God sent him here and he went back after his day was done. Why are you grieving, my brother?"

I said, "Lina Apa, we probably have all lost that true sensitivity. See? Where is that sense of loss after father's death? Where? None of us broke down in sorrow!"

Lina Apa's hand slipped from my head. She sat down on the mattress, silent, and looked at the sky.

I said again, "Tell me, why man goes on living? What is the use of living? What shall we ultimately gain? Life is a mirage, a lie. I am losing my faith in all values. What is the definition of life, Lina Apa? What does life offer us?"

She remained silent for a while, then said, "Sidhi, don't try to bind life by a definition. Life is life. You are all trying to circumscribe life within words, language, and definition. For thousands and thousands of years, life is going on, on this planet. Can we, within so short a life span, find a formula for life? Do you know what is the greatest mistake of people like you? You are trying to search for a meaning in life while standing outside life. Have you ever tried to live life? Life pure and simple. Try to live life without any definition and then see what happens?"

Lina Apa stopped to take a breath, then again continued, "Sidhi, one who sits on the steps of a pond dips his fingers in the cold water and shivers and cannot bathe. Even if he bathes, it is a hurried one and after waiting a long time. But one who jumps straight into the pond, without bothering about the cold, he really enjoys bathing. You intellectuals sitting on the steps of life fritter it away by trying to find a definition for it. When you begin to live, your time is gone; life does not wait to take something from you."

Lina Apa remained silent. I remained silent too. What answer could be given? I was always weak in argument; I was always in doubt. I could not choose the right path because I would always vacillate between right and wrong; between good and bad. So, I remained silent.

Lina Apa asked me, "Do you know, after father's death, who among us has become most helpless? Mother and me. We two feel that the ground under our feet has slipped away; the roof over our head is blown away. We two are the most unsafe. Mother is old. She can go and stay with any of her sons. She has at least some support from that quarter. But what support do I have? I am completely alone. This job is like the shadow of a palm tree. What shall I do after retirement? Who shall I depend on? Who will look after me? My brother will not give me shelter. Where shall I live then? This house will be in the possession of the brothers. Can I get shelter here? Think of my situation. I still go on living, even if completely alone. I am not running away from life because I know there is no running away. If you have to live, then why look for a definition? You have many duties. You have to continue Devedutta's education, bring him up. You have to write many more stories and novels. See, if you make the canvas of life wider, life becomes that much wider. We are accusing our brothers of selfishness because they have limited their duties and are living within the narrow bounds of their self-interest. If you run away from your duties because you are afraid of life, will not Devadutta think of you as selfish? Get up Sidhi, give up all this cynicism. Try to live life. Take it as a challenge."

I looked at Lina Apa doubtfully. "Can I? Can I really find my center of existence; the ground under my feet; the meaning of my life?"

Lina Apa's eyes looked as if she were saying, "You can Sidhi, you can. Come on Sidhi. Jump into the pond of life. How long can you sit there on the steps of life and be torn apart by the eternal conflict between yes and no? Get moving."

Can I really do it? I wanted to ask. Can I really stand up

with the strength of Arjun, pick up my bow and arrow, and face life?

But I could not utter a word. Lina Apa patted me on my back.

●●

The family priest consulted the almanacs and said two different almanacs were of two different opinions. One almanac found fault with the time of death; the other did not. Avinna came and enquired of the brothers if a special ceremony would be done to remove this fault on the time of death.

Eldest brother did not offer an opinion, only said to consult the others and decide. Manu Bhaina also avoided the issue. Somu Bhaina did not believe in rules and all that rubbish. Lina Apa said since so much money was being spent, why not add a little more and do that special ceremony. Nobody else offered a different opinion so it was decided to perform the special ceremony.

In the evening, Avinna came to make a list of things that would be required. Uncle was also called in. Mother too. Brothers were invited. They came and sat but did not participate in the discussion.

After the list for things required for feeding the Brahmins was made, another list for clothes to be given to all the members of the clan after the ceremonial bathing was also prepared. Mother, uncle, and Avinna, after discussion, decided only one member from a family would get a piece of clothing. In addition, all the relatives from outside would also each get a piece of clothing. All members of our family were included on the list except married brothers and their wives for whom dhoti and saree would come from their father-in-law's house. Manu Bhaina was included in our family list because nothing was expected from his father-in-law's side as we had cut off all relations with them. But at this point, Manu Bhaina said it was not necessary to buy clothes for him as it would come from his father-in-law's house. Mother was somewhat surprised and asked, "What do you mean? They have not been informed. Avinna, you were sending letters. Have you sent one to Manu's father-in-law?"

We had no relations with Manu Bhaina's father-in-law's family. They were not invited to any marriage function of ours. This time also, they were neither informed nor invited. So nobody thought of any gift from their side.

Manu Bhaina, head bent low, said in a grave voice, "I have informed them."

Mother only said, "Oh." There was a lot of meaning behind this small word and everybody understood. Silence all around. Nobody could say a word. Everybody was measuring himself in his own balance. Still something was going amiss. Maybe our method of measuring was wrong.

After a long silence Avinna said, "Now, let us complete the list. Then . . ."

The money Avinna was to lend us, he only gave us 500 rupees. In the market at Khunta, he was known to many of the shop keepers. We purchased all the clothes and groceries in his name on credit. It all came up to 2,500 rupees. Somu Bhaina, Devadutta, and I went with Avinna to do the marketing. The other brothers did not go; nobody had called them. But they probably expected to be called. I thought it was their duty. They should have come forward. They, however, stood on their prestige.

Sometimes I think we brothers and sisters were like those princes in the panchtantra story. The king had made all arrangements for the educations of his sons. Many pundits were engaged to teach different subjects. In the palace, these pundits in all their fury were moving about with big books in hand. Still, the king was not happy because even though his sons were well educated, they were lacking in practical common sense. They were always quarrelling, fighting, and shouting among themselves. On the slightest pretext they began to quarrel with the others. They thought of themselves as the worthiest human beings but they were slaves to their egos. Sometimes, they were made fools of by others and often cheated. Yet they did not learn anything. They did not know how to behave with others. They were unable to understand if their words hurt anybody. They did not know how to face problems or difficulties. That's why they were segregated from others and suffered.

Our brothers were just like that and Avinna made a profit out of it. He helped us buy things on credit worth 2,500 rupees and gave us 500 rupees in cash and made us agree to his condition if we could not return his 3,000 rupees at the end of three months, we would have to give him our best piece of land as payment.

This Avinna, at the time of father's illness, had hired a taxi and taken him to hospital at Baripada. It was this Avinna who lit the funeral pyre and was now observing the rituals. And yet how cleverly he bound us to his conditions. Our brothers were much better educated than Avinna. Eldest brother and Manu Bhaina were senior to him in age and experience but they lacked practical worldly knowledge. They would quarrel over trifles and would get angry when others would cheat them.

Take for instance Avinna. He was very sympathetic towards us. He did a lot at the time of father's death yet he did not forget his self-interest. Where was the true value of Avinna's sense of values? Selfishness hid behind all the show of love and affection. Everything else was hypocrisy and was for external show only.

After the quarrel, the three brothers formed a separate group. They whispered among themselves. Eldest brother-in-law was their advisor. I couldn't tolerate this man at all. I do not know why but whenever I saw that man, I felt his mind was always full of evil plans. And now he was now advising the three brothers, which meant something was going to happen.

Manu Bhaina had already left for Calcutta with the piece of bones. He would return on the tenth day after immersing the bone in the Ganges River. The piece of bone was then kept in the hollow of a peepal tree. Every evening a lamp was lit there. One day, I went to put the lamp there. Standing under the tree, I felt the last piece of evidence of father's body. I wanted very much to see that piece of bone but could not. I felt empty. Father's existence had vanished from the world except for this piece of bone. It was painful to think about.

••

"Nagendranath Pretayah." I was startled at these words. Father was now a preta, a ghost? Previously at the time of any ceremony the priest used to say "Nagendranath Barmanasya." I do not know if the word 'Barmana' signifies the warrior caste but at the time of Manu Bhaina's marriage, their priest had said "Manunath Dasasya" and for that, a quarrel erupted on the marriage pandal itself.

Now the priest said "Nagendranath Pretayah." It was painful to think of father as a ghost -- the father who was so dear to us, who was our progenitor, was now a ghost. Whereas I, a very disobedient son, was sitting on the steps of the pond watching the ceremony silently.

A tiny hut had been made on the edge of the pond. Avinna was cooking rice to be offered to the preta. The priest was nearby conducting the ceremony. A very tiny image was made of sand. It didn't have eyes, ears, or nose. A piece of father's bone was put inside that image. I was told Manu Bhaina had taken a very small piece of bone to be thrown into the Ganges; the rest would be used here. I was sitting there watching the ceremony. Avinna took a dip in the pond and coming up, offered the cooked rice to father. I was sitting there, my cheeks resting on my knees looking at father's image.

I, the fourth son of Nagendra Mohanty, sat there silently and watching Avinna praying for peace and liberation of father's soul. I felt very guilty. I began to feel father carried in his heart sorrow and a wounded feeling against everybody. He had left us without taking anything from us. How shall I repay his debt? How?

Father was talking incoherently while being taken to Baripada. He was helpless while calculating the expenses of only 50 rupees. What was the purpose of human life? Life was an empty dream. Here everyone was a stranger to everyone else. Brothers, sisters, father, mother, son, daughter; nobody was our own. All were hopelessly alone. What sort of a monument would man become living like this all alone? If that was the case, why should man continue to live?

Yet Lina Apa was talking of life. When I was with her, I felt she was living in spite of her helplessness. She was still living. I am not at all helpless compared with her. Why then should I not live? Those who think of life as meaningless, none of them commit suicide. Even a scholar writing a thesis on the philosophy of illusion forgets his philosophy while eating or when longing for love in the bed. Why then was there such a gap between living and looking for a meaning in life? Which was the right path? Which?

I was jolted out of my daydream at the sound of Avinna's voice reciting the mantra – my uncle, Nagendranath the ghost ....

On the tenth day, Avinna was to do the ceremony. But as a rule, eldest brother should have done it because he was the eldest. But he suffered from eosinophilia. His wife had already him warned he might catch cold if he took dips in the pond water ten times. Although she did say her husband wanted to do it, as, he said, the chance of offering prayer to father's departing spirit came only once in life. But if anything would happen to him, who would look after him? There was not even a doctor in the village.

Nobody then forced eldest brother. Manu Bhaina did not come forward either. None of us asked him to. Somu Bhaina did not believe in souls. He refused outright, saying all of that was superstition and he did not have this kind of emotionalism in his nature.

I argued, "Somu Bhaina, this may be superstitious and may be the result of emotionalism but a belief is involved in it. We are all ordinary people. We have something called a mind and a mind is a dangerous thing. We always remain guilty before it. Today you do not believe in these things but if tomorrow your belief changes, won't you regret that you did not do anything for father's funeral ceremony? After this tenth day, it will not come back. Can you then perform the ceremonies?"

Somu Bhaina retorted back, "It's because of this attitude that India is lagging behind. Man's life from beginning to end is a biological process. We already know that. We also know that there is no such thing as a soul, spirit, or self, whatever you call it. All this is the product of our beliefs, our traditions, and our past impressions.

Suppose at this moment, Lina Apa flared up and inquired, "You all are arguing about this? Sidhi, tell me, will you take the responsibility from Avinna to carry forward the proceedings or not?"

And I might answer, "If none of you come forward, I shall do it. I am father's youngest son. I have enough strength."

●●

Lina Apa said nothing more and a mini Mahabharat ensued, I said quickly, "I shall do that. I shall perform the rest of the ceremonies."

Lina Apa went on grumbling for some time more. Somu Bhaina got up and went to his wife. I was reminded of the "Princes of the Panchatantra" story and the students of Vishnu Sharma. In my family, all were educated but they didn't know what to speak, when, where, and how.

I was perturbed. Right from day one, everybody was unhappy. All were going about in a glum mood. None was prepared to tolerate the other. None was able to understand the other's pain. Everybody thought only of himself.

There was such a quarrel at the time of Somu Bhaina's marriage. Father called all the sons together and told them when few utensils were kept together, there was bound to be some friction. That was a very common thing; it happened in every family. Daughters-in-law had come from different families. At first, they would find it difficult to pull on together. But you are all brothers; you are of the same blood. You have grown up together from your childhood. Why were you not able to live together amicably? Everybody remained silent before father. All sat there with their heads bowed.

Now father was no more. Who would call them together and explain when the utensils were thrown together, they would produce some jarring noise? Who else was there before whom everybody would bow their heads?

I had a sharp pain in my head. I was going away. What I heard from the other room was Somu Bhaina being scolded by his wife in a subdued voice. "What family is mad . . . . I could not totally hear Somu Bhaina's voice. I came away and went into the courtyard.

After the ninth-day ceremony, in the evening, I took the responsibility from Avinna and was prepared to go through the whole process. Avinna took me to a corner in the house and said, "You will sleep near this doorsill tonight. Will you be afraid? A laborer will be sleeping near you. This pot is meant for the ghost; there is lamp burning inside. See that it does not go out. You and the laborer will take turns and watch over the flame throughout the night. I have told the laborer both of you will go out early in the morning and sit under the banyan tree at the end of the village. So that none in the house see your face when you go out, leave the house when it is still dark."

A majhi caste young man, who was a servant in our family, and I, early in the morning on the tenth day, went and sat under the banyan tree. As soon as the sun came up, the majhi boy left me and went to his house. I remained there learning against the tree. From time to time, I would push up the wick in the lamp a little. I would have to sit the whole day under this tree. By the time they would finish bathing, it would be two or three o'clock.

The banyan tree was not very far from our own house. I could see it from where I sat and could hear people inside the house talking. A peculiar trait in middle-class families -- especially in lower middle-class families -- was to talk loudly. The house would be never tranquil throughout the day. It was as if they had never learned to speak softly.

Tomorrow the Brahmins would be fed. Today the big hearths would be prepared. Avinna must be busy for that. Invitations were to be sent out to the Brahmins, making arrangements for the feast. Avinna had to do everything in this regard. My brothers, sitting on their beds and taking care of their children, would be gossiping with their wives.

Lina Apa and Devadatta would be working too but would be getting irritated. This was a bad trait in own family. No one tolerated the other. Father used to say, "It is not a house, but a sheep yard." Once father as so annoyed that he blurted out, "there will be peace in this house only after my death." But that peace abided us even after his death.

That Majhi boy who had gone home came back with my toothbrush, toothpaste, tea in a flask, and a mug of water and reported, "Apa said that you won't eat anything today. Only drink tea; Apa has given a whole bottle for you."

But I did not feel like washing my face. I went on sitting there, seeing me sitting unmoving, the Majhi boy said, "Why don't you drink the tea? What shall I tell Apa?"

I told him to go home as there must be work to do and I would wash my face when I felt like it.

Nunu Bhai returned from Calcutta by noon. From Khunta bus stop, he came straight to the banyan tree. He couldn't enter the house before the ceremonial haircut and bath. He too sat down with me. Obligatory gifts from the families of Somu Bhaina and eldest brother's father-in-law's house were delivered. Nunu Bhaina asked the men carrying the gifts what had been given and from whom.

Next came younger uncle who had a job at Tata and father's elder brother's son who was living at Khadagpur. They too sat down with us. Younger uncle sent word through a cowherd boy of their arrival. That boy brought cold drinks for us.

The barber came still later. Uncle, because he was annoyed, asked him to go home and told everybody to come out soon.

The barber told us they were all waiting for the gifts from Manu Bhaina's father-in-law's house. As soon as they came, they would all come out.

Then younger uncle enquired about our family duties: who had taken change of the cooking for tomorrow; what were the things purchased; how many Brahmins were invited etc.

By the time all came out of the house, it was two in the afternoon. Seeing Avinna, younger Uncle said to him, "O Avinna, why did you make the ceremonies so late? When will the ceremonies begin? When would everybody shave their moustaches and beards? How long would the small children wait without food?"

Avinna was red with anger. He looked back to see who was there and who was not. Seeing eldest brother, Manu Bhaina, Somu Bhaina, and eldest brother-in-law coming together he snarled, "See those three sons of uncle? Those bastards have come to the marriage party of Nagendra Mohanty."

Uncle hushed him by saying he was quite grown up but did not yet know how to talk.

Later, I heard Manu Bhaina waited for the gift from his father-in-law's house. He was sure somebody would be coming but none came. That was why it was late. In the end, it was decided Manu Bhaina and his wife would take the dhoti and Saree bought for Mina Apa and her husband but there was nothing for their children. So Avinna had to run again to Khunta market and buy clothes for the children. It was because of all this farce that it became late.

After everybody gathered near the pond, the ceremonies began. I cooked, took a dip in the pond, offered food to the ghost, and recited "Mama Pitah Nagendranath Pretayah," my father the ghost.

After this, the barber cut our hair, shaved us, and manicured our nails. Avinna too did all this because he had lit the funeral pyre. By the time everything was over and we returned home, it was close to sunset. On the way, I marked after shaving our heads, we all looked different. It was as if we had gone back to our childhood days.

After returning from the funeral ceremony at the pond, we

washed our feet, sprinkled Ganga water over our heads, and entered the house. We heard in our absence, there has been another Mahabharat. The reason for this was the barber's wife had manicured the fingernails of all the ladies and all the children. Then they took their bath in the family pond. Then Manu Bhaina's children complained their pants and shirts were not their size; instead, they were a little smaller. Elder brother's children too demanded better clothes than what had come from their grandfather's house. So all the children were standing there naked after their bath; they would not listen to any pleadings from their mothers. Manu Bhaina's wife got angry and started beating her children. Lina Apa and the other two sisters-in-law dragged the children away and scolded their mothers mildly. They said, "They are children; they can't understand these things. Why should you beat them? Try to make them understand."

Middle sister-in-law was still angry and scolding her children. Then she said to eldest sister-in-law, "What shall we do, sister? These children have never put on such cheap clothes. It is my misfortune that they have to put on clothes meant for the children of servants and laborers."

Lina Apa was hurt by these words and as was her usual manner, she retorted angrily. So this was the cause of the farce.

Everybody became serious again. I saw mother sitting, leaning against the wall. Tears were running down her cheeks. She was looking upward vacantly. Tears from her eyes were running to her ears. A pitiful scene. My eyes too began to water. I ended up leaving the area.

I was standing there holding on to the edge of the thatched roof when a post card dropped down, perhaps disturbed by my hand. I picked it up and saw it was from Divyendu Bhaina. When had it come? Did someone read it and put it there? I did not know. So, I read it. He had written that Mina Apa wouldn't be coming to the funeral ceremony as her due date was very near. He too could not go leaving her alone. In spite of all the noise, I was dragged into a world of silence. A kind of unknown sorrow sprouted in my heart. Why? For whom? What kind of sorrow was this? Was it for Mina Apa or for her absence? That was what the world was. Man didn't have the freedom to turn back.

Before the communal dinner that night, there was another quarrel regarding the choice of the location for another ceremony of purification. Lina Apa and Avinna were of the opinion the last resting place where father slept before going to hospital at Baripada should be the place for the ceremony. But Manu Bhaina and eldest brother-in-law were currently staying there. They suggested the place in the drawing room where I had slept last night. Their argument was since the ceremony of pushkar would be held at midnight, the children would be afraid at the sight so it should be held in a corner.

Avinna and Lina Apa stuck to their opinion. Since it was for the benefit of father's soul, it should be done at the place father last slept. Over this small affair, another quarrel erupted. Eldest brother-in-law said angrily it was his last visit to his father-in-law's home.

I was listening to them silently but finally could not control myself anymore. How selfish they all had become Father's death was not affecting them at all. They all were thinking of their own self-interest. I said angrily, "Have you all been invited to father's marriage party? You are all right except you have lost your humanity." Eldest brother-in-law took offence to this; he felt he had been hit directly. He got up, went to his wife and said he did not want to stay in that house anymore. He would leave as soon as the ceremony was over. Later on, it was decided that Manu Bhaina and eldest brother-in-law would sleep in Nunu Bhaina's room for that night.

The quarrels subsided for the time being as everybody was busy at the communal feast. Mother was sitting there in the dark as before, leaning against the wall, eyes unseeing, deaf and dumb. Eldest sister, finding mother alone as everybody was busy, went and sat down with her and poured out her sorrow.

It did not escape the notice of Lina Apa. In spite of being

busy, she took me to a corner and said, "Sidhi, see eldest sister's common sense? In the condition mother is in, she is saying that after father's death, her husband was no more honored in this house. We brothers and sisters are misbehaving with him. In this house, she said younger ones are not showing proper respect to elder ones. This house will break up very soon," she said.

After giving me a litany of elder sister's complaints, Lina Apa said, "Now tell me, Sidhi, what is the purpose of telling all these to mother at such a time of sorrow? Will it not give her more pain?"

Before I could say anything, she went inside and told her, "You don't have any common sense, elder sister. Why are you telling these things to mother at such a time?"

Inevitably, this turned into a serious disagreement. The three sisters-in-law took the weeping elder sister inside. Eldest and middle sisters-in-law were very much upset about this, so much so it prompted eldest sister-in-law to say, "You just wait. When the time comes, I shall break her back with a kick. Otherwise, I am not the daughter of So-and-so Patnaik."

This quarrel slowly made its way from the inside to the outside. It must have given a lot of pain to Lina Apa for she cried for a long time, sitting in the dark with her head between her knees.

It was not that I did not feel hurt by these words of elder sister-in-law either but my anger transferred itself to elder brother. I wondered how he did not scold his wife even once. What an effeminate fellow! I felt like rushing up to him and saying, "Aren't you ashamed? Being hen-pecked by her! Fie, you put on the saree and bangles and she'll wear the pants."

But I contained my anger within myself. Lina Apa stopped too after 15 minutes of crying. She wiped her tears and did what she was doing, but she too could not resist the temptation and said, "Listen Avinna, a middle school pass woman is saying that she would break my back by kicking me. She does not know that I am qualified enough to teach her husband."

Avianna pacified her and suggested, "Wait, 'til all this is over. Then we will see who loses in her bid to break her own sister's back. We are a family of Kankas, not Majhi or Chamars. Come let us go. There is so much to see done yet."

This conversation between Lina Apa and Avinna was immediately transmitted to the ladies inside.

After the communal feast, all the leftovers were put in a pot. Avina, Devadutta and I carried it and with a bamboo stick in hand, proceeded towards the end of the village.

Avinna asked me "Sidhi, can you carry this pot? Remember, you have to carry it without stopping on the way."

I gave him an affirmative shake of my head and lifted the pot. Avinna and Devadutta followed me with the stick and a lantern. At the end of the village under a palm tree, Avinna put the pot on the ground and lighting a lamp, bowed. We did the same. By then, it was midnight. The village was absolutely quiet. Only the chirping of crickets was heard sometimes and somewhere, a stray dog was barking.

Avinna said, "I shall break the pot by one stroke of the stick. Then we will go home without looking back." Then he struck the pot very hard.

When we reached home, we found the door closed from the inside. Avinna thumped the thatch with the stick. Lina Apa, from the inside, asked, "Who is it?"

Avinna said, "We visited the sacred places. We went to the river Ganga, Goddabari, Kashi, and Gaya and then, we bowed down to Lord Jagannath. Now we have returned."

Lina Apa then asked, "What did you donate at the sacred places and what have you brought back?"

Avinna replied, "We gave up our sorrows and brought happiness. What are you doing inside?"

Lina Apa replied, "We are chewing iron Chickpeas."

Avinna asked, "Won't you give us some?"

Lina Apa replied, "Then come inside."

Avinna pushed open the door and went inside. All this was

new to me. I had never seen this ceremony. Lina Apa called us inside; Devadutta and I went inside. Sill rice powder was sprinkled on the door. Lina Apa bent down and observing the rice powder, said, "See the mark of feet of a bird."

Mother questioned, "Lina, your father will be reborn as a bird?"

Avinna commented, "Aunty, bird life is much better than human life. Birds have no sorrow."

When Lina Apa was observing the fact mark on the sprinkled rice powder, elder brother and Samu Bhaina lay on their beds and whispered something to their wives.

This particular ceremony called, Puskar Shanti, I had never seen before, nor had Devadutta. Mother and Lina Apa asked Devadutta to go and sleep but he did not budge. For the ceremony, the cot was made to stand on its two legs. The place was screened off. On this side of the screen Devadutta, mother, Lina Apa, and I slept on a mattress. An image was made of rice and black gram. Avinna showed us the image and told us it would be worshiped by the burning of ghee and the singing of songs. "There is nothing more to see. You go now and sleep on the other side and listen."

Two Brahmins and Avinna conducted the ceremony. We four sat on the side which was dark. The Brahmin sang his song to the tune of a tambouta:

Bones of Your breast
Piece by piece
Will be shared
By jackal and Hyenas to eat.

I again plunged into my helplessness of what exactly was fulfillment in a man's life? This materialistic civilization in which our life was enmeshed in the culture of consumerism, how brittle was this life? These my brothers, who think of nothing else, but their own families, had they ever stopped to think why all these quarrels and why this push and pull of self-interest? Who was mine and who was not? Wife, son, daughter -- nobody will accompany you! This tape recorder; the house in Budhheswari colony; sofa set; fridge; motorcycle; costly clothes. Nothing was really yours. Why then was man always running after them? Why was man so assiduously looking for happiness? What exactly was this experience of happiness? What happiness had elder brother achieved? Or Manu Bhaina? Elder brother was a communist in his college days and was a member of SFI. He was dreaming of socialism. Where had that dream gone? Where was that idealistic young man lost? Today he was replaced by a corrupt, selfish government official. Ask him what happiness had he got when he smiled in self-satisfaction looking at his half-built home in Buddheswari Colony? Ask him what would he take with him at the end? Why would anybody remember him after his death? Who would say such a man was once alive?

We created a family for the desire of immortality within us. He wanted to leave something of himself in his children so that people would remember him after his death. But who would remember him after his death? Who remembers whom? Who would remember our own father by looking at us? What have we done to keep alive father's name?

Much better it was to devote oneself to literature; to let your whole life be spent in the service of literature. People would remember you even after your death. It didn't matter if you were deprived of worldly happiness -- tape recorder, TV, sofa set, Godrej shelves, and a house in Budheswari colony. These things were of no value. Two meals of watered rice a day was enough.

Still there were some questions which remained. If all this TV, sofa set, etc. were worthless, why then was man always running after them? We could go back to the Stone Age, stay in caves, could live on half-boiled animal flesh. If I was asked to go back to that age, could I? If I didn't share for two days, I felt uncomfortable. Without newspapers for two days, I felt suffocated. Could one live without these? Could one live without trains, buses, or airplanes? Our speech and our writing also were the gifts of that civilization which was dragging us into consumerism. We couldn't do without all those ingredients of enjoyment, yet we wanted to abolish all this culture of consumerism. This simply was not possible.

Man lived for a moment in time; he was not immortal. All those elements of enjoyment would be useless for him after that short period. Then why should man run after them for as long as he lived? Would he accept this culture of consumerism?

Then I would be forced to be like elder brother and Manu Bhaina. This culture of consumerism made us inhuman. If we followed it, we would be like animals. How would we humanize this animal? How would we give up this culture of consumerism? How should we turn back from this materialistic civilization and return to spirituality? It then would become necessary to go back to the Stone Age.

No. Don't talk to me about finding the middle paths. They were not practical; they were only ideals and I hate ideals with all my heart. What was man's intrinsic nature? Don't tell me 'it should be like this.' Tell me clearly whether to walk on this side of the road or on the other side of the road. On this middle of the road, I sometimes leaned to this side or to that without my knowledge. Which side was right? Which?

As if all the nerves of my brain were going to pieces, I threw out all thought and came back to my normal state. Mother was sleeping with her arm on her eyes, certainly not asleep. Was she weeping? She had lived with father for the last 40 or 45 years. Could she forget all those memories?

Lina Apa was sitting leaning against the wall. From the corner of her still eyes, tears were rolling down her cheeks. They were glistening in the dim light. Devadutta was sitting with his head between his knees. All the others were probably asleep. Only the sound of the priest's voice was heard. We four were helpless creatures, sitting in the dark, trying to find a way out. Which road was right? Which road would lead us towards life? Where should we get the proof of our existence? Where would we be safe? On which road would we find the ground under our feet? Which road?

I patted Devadutta's head. He could not control himself anymore. He pushed against me and his tears soaked my breast. None of us was speaking. Sorrow had no language nor was it necessary. I too couldn't control my tears.

The next morning Avinna took me aside and said, "I don't find the situation happy. Something has to be done."

At first, I could not understand anything. I asked him, "What are you talking about? What do we have to do?"

Avinna's face hardened in excitement. He explained "Yesterday after uncle's death, elder sister-in-law is saying that she would break Lina's back. And our effeminate brother is silent. Tell me, what will happen to Lina after your mother's death? She will be kicked around by brothers and their wives? Why, what hasn't she got? She has read so much. Which girl in our village has got an MA degree? The daughter-in-law of this house are not equal even to the little finger on her left hand. Why are they threatening her? What gives them courage to dream of making her their maidservant?"

It was not that I was not hurt by elder sister-in-law's words yesterday. But I did not want to make it an issue because of the pressure of work. I was amazed elder brother could listen to this silently. I responded, "I don't see any way out. If elder brother does not restrain his wife . . ."

Avinna replied, "Phew, that effeminate fellow won't do anything. Whatever has to be done will be done by us. Tonight, after the Brahmins are fed, call for a meeting. There you put forward the proposal that all the land be transferred to mother and Lina Apa's name. After aunty, Lina will be the owner of that property. If Lina gets married then the property would revert back to the five brothers. Sidhi, I don't see any other way out. Lina and aunty need at least a roof over their heads."

Later, I went and told of this proposal to Lina Apa. She at first refused and said, "I don't need all these. I don't want this property."

"You don't understand Lina Apa." I tried to make her

understand the importance of this. I said, "Remember what happened last night? What a nasty thing elder sister-in-law said? Elder brother remained silent. Father died only yesterday and today, she says such nasty things. After Mother's death she may be nastier than this. Why? Why should you give up the land under your feet? Why should you not think of your future?"

She remembered what happened last night and her mind changed from softness to hardness. She said, "I don't have any objection. But will the brothers agree?"

Then I went to mother and told her about it. At first, she did not understand. After I explained to her the pros and cons, she asked, "Will I have the right over the land?"

I then explained to her she would get half of the property as long as she was alive; the other half would belong to Lina Apa. After her death, Lina Apa would get the all of it. She then agreed to a meeting after the feast for the Brahmins.

I sat down to do the ritual. But I could not keep my mind under control. Always the thought came to me I was going to complete what father left half-done. Father was most worried about Lina Apa. He always felt guilty for not getting her married off. That's why he loved Lina Apa so much. He used to accept all her scolding with a smile. He used to break down thinking of Lina Apa's future. I am going to solve that problem today. This would be the greatest offering to him. What greater offering could be made for the peace of his soul?

Then the priest reciting his mantra said "Nagendranath Bramanyasya" instead of "Nagendranath Pretaya," I closed my eyes in happiness.

After the feast, brothers, their wives, elder sister and her husband fell over each other in offering honorariums to the priests. The Brahmins were surprised and happy. It was not one, but four of five persons were offering honorariums. Lina Apa brought some one-rupee notes and gave them to Devadutta and I to give to the Brahmins and thereby earn some holy righteousness.

After this, I met everyone and asked them to attend a meeting as that was mother's wish. The meeting was held in the courtyard. Uncle was given a stringed cot to sit on. Beside him sat elder brother, Manu Bhaina, Somu Bhaina, and elder brother-in-law. On the outer veranda, Avinna, Devadutta and I sat. Mother and Lina Apa stood near the door. Sisters-in-law stood half hidden behind the doors.

I began the topic. I talked about the maintenance of the property, mother's future, and finally came to the point about transferring the property to mother and Lina's name.

Elder sister made it clear from the beginning she had nothing to do with the property. She was not here to stake a claim to it.

Other brothers probably could not decide at first how to begin. After a brief silence, Somu Bhaina said, "I protest. I don't agree. Today I have a job. Tomorrow if I lose my job, where shall I go? Refugee?"

Avinna said, "Today Lina has a job. Tomorrow if she loses her job, where will she go?"

Somu Bhaina said, "Why, in this house?"

Avinna said angrily, "She will stay here to become your maid servant? And your wives will break her back by kicking?"

Somu Bhaina said with some levity, "Why, she too will have an equal share."

This time Avinna laughed and said, "My dear boy, you have been away for far too long while studying and then working. Do you know how much land you have in the village? Hundreds of acres, is that not it? If you had that much land, uncle would not have gone mad at the last moment trying to reconcile 50 rupees' worth of expenses. Now listen and remember: you have only four acres and ten gunthas of land. You are five, your mother and Lina, altogether six. Do you know how much your share will be if divided by six? That much land even a beggar has."

This time Somu Bhaina became adamant and said, "Whatever it may be, I cannot forego my claim on the land."

Elder brother too said he could not forego his claim either.

Land was not important. It was the memory. Father's memory was there; he would not give it up.

I could not control myself any longer. My whole body was burning with anger. Avinna shouted, "I will see who will come here to take his share of the property. You will build your own house in Bhubaneswar, buy tape recorder, ride on motorcycle, spend your time and money in luxury and comfort, and then once a year, you will come to take your share? Uncle left this land for that? How selfish you all are! You are not prepared to give away even an inch of land to your own sister? What education have you received? Wearing trousers and shirts of polyester cloth does not make you educated. Your heart and mind are all black. Fie, fie."

Elder brother got up and shouted back at Avinna, "Who, who are you? Get out you bastard. Get out. It is my house. Mine. My property. Who the hell are you to tell us this rubbish? Get out."

I was smoldering in anger and shot back at him, "You son of a bitch." I could not control myself any longer. I knew if I stayed, I may say bad things. My mind was filled with hatred towards elder brother. When I left the meeting, I gave a hard kick to the veranda out of all the anger, hatred, and distress I felt within. A hinge on it had dislodged but nobody noticed it. The last and the severest Mahabharat of this house was going to be fought here. The whole street was agog. All the neighbors were listening. I bent down my head in shame, what a sorry state of affairs this was. All our honour and dignity had been lost. Quarreling like Majhis and Chamars, a sheep yard. Father's words came to mind: "Four utensils put together will produce a jarring noise. That is normal. We shall not fight over that."

Why did I do this today? I called elder brother a son of a bitch? Fie on me! If father were alive today, he would have seen how his educated sons were fighting for a few gunthas of land which ultimately would be of no use to them. This was like the fighting among the Jadu clan -- the last fight. Were we all the last remnant of the Jadu clan?

When I returned home at about midnight, Lina Apa was sitting near the hearth resting her cheeks on her knees. Devadutta was eating. The entire house was silent. Everybody had gone quiet. The lantern was burning feebly.

Lina Apa said to me, "Sit. Take your dinner. Mother did not eat anything. I managed to make her drink a little warm milk. I have eaten."

Devadutta protested. "No. She is lying. She has not eaten."

Lina Apa said to him sharply, "You finish your meal and go to sleep." Then serving me dinner she said, "What was the necessity of creating this ruckus? What will people think? Everybody will blame me? Not you."

I could not say anything. After dinner I snuck away silently. Mother was sleeping. I put my hand on her head. She asked "Who, Sidhi?"

When I was patting her head, she wept loudly. She lamented, "All three of my sons and the eldest son-in-law are insisting on leaving tomorrow. They say they have no rights any more in this house. You know, before the thirteenth day, nobody leaves the house. They have children and their families if anything bad were it happen? They say they have no relations with this house anymore. What a thing to say! I am your mother. I have carried each of you for nine months. You are forgetting me! These few acers of land are everything! This house does not include me? How could you say such a thing?"

Mother cried out loudly. I tried to pacify her. Devadutta who was sleeping with her got up and said, "Don't cry, mama. Please don't cry. We are here with you. We are your sons and daughters."

Mother wiped her tears and said in a wounded voice, "I know, I know. I have seen you all. 'til you are married, you are all mine. The moment you get married, I become a nobody. Then, your wife is everything to you. That is my misfortune too." Mother again started crying, loudly. All her distress and all her tears were flowing like a stream.

There was a group photo in my album. It was taken in a

studio before my birth with father and mother sitting. Mamu Bhaina and Lina Apa were standing beside them. In the back, eldest brother and eldest sister were standing. Meena Apa and Somu Bhaina were sitting in front at their feet. Eldest brother was about 14 or 15 years old. Eldest sister and Lina Apa sat on the floor. Two pigtails were hanging. It was an old-fashioned photograph, turning yellow. Still I could not get rid of it. Underneath it, I have written, "hanging banyan roots."

Forty or 55 years ago, a young man of 19 had taken the hand of a girl of 15 or 16 with a lot of excitement and some dreams. I do not have a photo from that time in my album. But I have now reached the age when I can understand that time and experience the excitement in their hearts. I could now understand how many dreams he must have harbored when he went to Gorumahisani with mother. Today, everything was in ruins. That tree which was growing between dream and reality for the last 40 years was now cut down. Its branches and trunk were now in pieces. Early in the morning, brothers, their wives, and eldest sister were making their preparations to leave. I was woken up by the sounds of their feet, by their whispers, and by their packing of luggage. Ever since, I had been thinking of those things. I know mother, Lina Apa, and Devadutta were awake on their beds. Everyone could hear the sounds of a house being broken down. All relationships, all values were breaking down as well.

Lina Apa got up quickly and went to the kitchen and prepared tea. After straining the tea, she came to eldest brother and said, I have prepared tea. Please drink it."

Eldest brother was somewhat shy and said, "Why did you take the trouble to make tea so early in the morning? We could have taken our tea at Baripada." After a brief silence, he said, "All right, if you have made it, then give me some" Eldest brother, Somu Bhaina, and his wife drank some tea; the others did not. Eldest sister-in-law said to second sister-in-law quoting a proverb, "So much affection during the day, but in the darkness of night, stabbing."

I thought Lina Apa would be annoyed at this, that there would be another quarrel at the time of their departure. But Lina Apa kept calm.

Mother called eldest brother and said, "This is the twelfth day. Can't you postpone for another day? You have small children; it is not good for them to leave now."

Eldest brother said with all humility, "I don't have any more leave. What can I do?"

Mother again said "What is the urgency to start at dawn? You could wait till the sun is up."

Eldest brother, again with the same humility, said, "I have some work at Baripada."

Mother did not insist anymore. She understood a tree once cut down cannot be made to stand again; it would fall down without fail. She sighed and remained silent.

Everyone, after putting their luggage together before leaving, came to mother and touched her feet. She was sitting on the bed as before. She blessed them all and said the same thing to all: "Be happy. After reaching your place, write to me. Take care of your health."

Her voice was unusually tender and compassionate now. Every word was coming from the depth of her heart. Her voice was now wet with tears of kindness.

I was reminded of father. He used to tell us a story when we were children. The hero of the story wanted to marry a princess but she had a condition: the one who could bring his mother's heart and offer it to her would be her husband. The hero, after seeing the princess wanted so much to marry her, he almost became insane. But the condition, mother's heart had to be offered. He could not decide what to do. In desperation, he rushed home and killed his mother and rushed back with her heart. When he arrived, he was breathless because of running nonstop. On the way, he stumbled and the heart fell from his hand. He was not aware of his own pain. Hurriedly, he tried to pick it up but stopped dead when the heart said, "My dear boy, are you hurt?"

Mother's words were as tender as those of the heart. My brothers probably did not care. These are matters of sentiment. Why should they be so sentimental? Everybody touched mother's feet and went on their way. Our regular servant had brought with him two more Majhi boys; they all carried the luggage.

After everybody had left, Lina Apa closed the door and came back. The four of us were sitting on the bed, almost dumb. Each one was deep in his/her own thoughts. 'til yesterday, the house was full of noise and bustle. Today, it was empty and silent.

After a long time, mother said as if to herself, "In the meeting that day, everybody was eager to take me with them. Today nobody asked me where I shall stay or what I shall do." Mother's words were as tender as before. None of us could say anything. All were silent. The sun was rising.

After sunrise, Devadutta discovered Manu Bhaina had thrown the new clothes he and his family had been given into a corner.

In the evening uncle, Avinna, mother, Lina Apa, and myself decided it would not be right to leave mother alone in the village. So Lina Apa would take mother with her. The land would be rented and Avinna would look after it. We would come home from time to time to look after the house. Besides, during vacation, Lina Apa and mother would come and stay in the village.

Cattle would be looked after by the Majhi boy and at night, he would sleep at the house. All those things were decided in the presence of uncle, Avinna, mother, and Lina Apa. Household goods were locked up in one room and double-locked. The veranda was left for the servant boy.

On the fourteenth day of father's death, mother, Lina Apa, Devadutta, and I left the house. Did anyone even think 14 days ago we would have to leave the house? Even if we stayed at a distance, we always had the assurance we had a village and a home we could go to and stay there whenever we liked because father and mother were there. Today, we had lost that assurance. We became refugees. Our village address had been lost.

Father, after leaving the job at Gorumahisani, came and built this house. It was a big house. For two persons, it was difficult to maintain such a big house. Mother sweeping the rooms became tired and used to grumble and complain to father about its large size. Besides, in so big a house, father and mother probably felt lonely. So every time, they would ask one of us to come and to stay there. But we sons never cared for that.

Today, all our relationships with that house were being cut asunder. That house where mother had left the imprint of her memories of the past 15 or 16 years. Mother had entered into this house for the first time after doing the ritual worship. Forty or 45 years ago, mother had come to this village as a new bride with an adolescent mind. At that time, she must have felt deeply satisfied. Today she was leaving that house and that village, leaving behind all memories, all past, and all experiences.

Locking the house mother's eyes brimmed with tears. When she told Avinna, "Avinna, I leave the house behind, look after it for me." She could not control her tears anymore. Her voice shook. Lina Apa wiped her own eyes with her handkerchief.

Lina Apa had an Agfa camera with her and took photos of the house from many different angles. In this courtyard, eldest brother's, Manu Bhaina's, Somu Bhaina's, and Meena Apa's marriage were held. Here, the marriage mandap had been set up, and petromax lights had been lit. This courtyard was witness to some joy and happiness and some disappointment and sorrow. When I came to the village in the evening, I slept here and my watch would descend slowly. In the distance somewhere, a water hen cried out and the cuckoo chirped its special sounds. Birds flew away to their nests with some haste. From the neighboring home, my cousin sisters sung the evening prayer.

O Lord Jagannath, I am not asking for anything, neither riches nor children. I only ask for a little space in your sacred sands.

Listening to that prayer I plunged into a kind of strange happiness. Wherever I may be, whenever I remember the village, such memories flooded my mind of the memory of an evening, soft and sweet. It would probably never come again in my life. Sleeping in the courtyard, I would never again listen to the prayer of my cousin sisters which would lift me up much above common experiences. Never again would I have that good fortune.

Before leaving the house, Lina Apa took a pinch of dust from the courtyard and pasted it on her forehead. Mother pressed her saree to her eyes to suppress her tears. Avinna reassured mother, "Aunty, don't worry, I shall take care of this house! You come every summer vacation."

By the time we reached the Baripada bus stop, the buses for Tata and Balasore were already waiting. Lina Apa asked me. "When will you reach Rourkela?"

I said, "I have to catch the Howrah Bombay express. It reaches Tata by about 4:30 p.m. and will reach Rourkela by about nine."

Mother said, "After reaching Rourkela, write to us. Take care of your health and send money in time to Debu."

Both the buses blew their horns. I helped mother and Lina Apa to get into the bus for Bhadrak. Lina Apa said, a little worried, "Your bus will leave, Go."

Devadutta and I both bent down to touch their feet. Lina Apa and mother advised Devadutta to live carefully. I came back to board my bus, when Devadutta came and touched my feet. I patted his shoulder. Lina Apa poked her head out of the window and said, "Write to me Sidhi. Come to Balasore when you have the time."

I said to Devadutta, "Write to me, Debu. Read mindfully. I shall send you money in time. Your studies will not stop after father's death. They will continue for sure."

Tears flowed freely from Devadutta's eyes. While trying to wipe away his tears, my own eyes brimmed with tears as well. Suddenly I felt – no, no, even if an earthquake had shattered the values of love, affection, and faith, still all was not lost. Something was still alive in our hearts. I rushed back to the bus for Bhadrak and said, "Mother, you write to me. And take care of your health."

What else could be said? I felt I wanted to tell mother a lot more. But what? Many things were churning inside my heart. I didn't know what they were. I could never express them in spoken words. They were deeply felt experiences, inexpressible. Ah! If only I could hold mother in my arms and cry, that would have lightened my heart.

The bus for Tata blew its horn; I got into the bus. The bus started rolling. I poked my head out of the windows and looked. The bus for Balasore was also blowing its horn. It was an alert to leave. I waved my hand farewell. From that side, two palms of love and affection waved back but stayed behind in the private bus which started at Baripada.

THE TIGER

Dear readers, a helpless lamentation of soundless distress is hidden in this story. Be interested. Advance slowly towards the story. Throw away the words, take away ornaments of poetry. Scratch away the thin layer of words, dig deep and uproot them to reach the depth. Blow away the similes and metaphors. Then you will see a helpless distress lying supine, without a covering. That is our goal.

Come, it will take you to an unfamiliar world where your politics and election, hunger and exploitation do not exist. There is no love, no attachment, nor tears, nor taste of a kiss. Yet all these are there – in different forms and with different tastes. There you will meet raw nature in every atom, every molecule. You will meet the whole universe. It will take you beyond millions of light years to another universe.

●●

Many thought of him as uneducated and uncultured, without any experience and sensibility, an inert piece of clod – Jada Bharat. He had no politics, no sense of discrimination between good and bad. He did not know love and affection, had no attachment to anything. He had not benefited by a dish antenna nor did he understand the language of Star TV. So, he did not know what love was. From time immemorial he was not even a man for the Odia readers of stories. He was an animal of flesh and blood, of arteries and veins, of bones and bone marrow, of hair on the skin and head, of nails and teeth, of eyes and ears, and a nose. He had only a stomach, no brain. Such ideas were wrapped round him so that his real appearance was not visible to Odia readers.

Yet beneath all those layers was hidden his real character; like Valmiki, like Ratnakara, merciless in killing, soft in death, cool in judgment, hot in love. Come, I will take you to such a man. Come, he was sitting on the bond of the pond. The chameleon had appeared by shaking its head thrice. The forgetful dragonfly would be dragged away to its depth by the tongue of the frog. Come, come quickly.

Where lied hidden so much hunger? Only hunger made him restless. He had eaten a few date palm fruits mixed with sand, more skin and seed than kernel. He had eaten three guavas – no not three, only two-and-a-half because a part of one had been shared by a bat. Before he could eat another, an urchin saw him and shouted. That urchin was as faithful as Hanuman. While eating guava, did he not remember his hungry son or his starving wife or his old mother suffering from an unknown disease? No, not at all. It was not that all human sensibility was wasted away. It was not when he took his son on his lap he didn't not feel any attachment. It was not that philosophers made him tired and exhausted by throwing him like a tennis ball between existentialism and socialism. For what pleasure did a self-banished man go to the forest, pick up a rifle, and let blood flow from a heart? A status quoits became a terrorist? Discarding Lenin's garment, people now took up Gorbachev's or Yeltsin's instead?

For his wife only he had the raw passion of midnight. It was not he didn't turn to God and pray to be spared this dreadful fate when he was carrying your mother to the cremation ground. But he could not assuage his hunger. And this was also true in this world, there was no unadulterated truth.

There he was, sitting hidden on the bond of the pond. The minister would come to the college to erect a pandal. He was requested to contribute his labor by some students of the college, by lecturers, and by some gentlemen of the village. He had made up his mind not to go. He did not feel at all inclined to work, neither free labor nor bonded labor at the village headman's, nor even paid work in the field. He did not like to muck around in the watery mud nor among paddy plants, insects and grass and creepers. Rather, he liked to sit on the bond between fields and watch the struggles of life – how the bonds were being washed away by the current, how helpless the insects were during a storm, or how a school of small fish, against all odds, swam in procession to declare their victory.

Come, come to him. Tear away the skin from his bare chest. See how he has kept himself imprisoned in the chamber of bones with windows closed and screened. Was he sweating profusely? Was he feeling suffocated? Wait a second. Once you get acclimated to the darkness, everything would be visible. So clear in the mirror would your face appear. Come, jump into the chamber of his heart.

Very irritating and very horrifying was the dream. A tiger was waiting in the courtyard. They all were behind closed doors under a low thatched roof. There were four of them, very uncomfortable in the smoke and spider webs. The old mother was almost unconscious, covered with rags, and whimpering on the floor. He was trying to see the tiger through the chinks in the door of bamboo splints. Surunani and her son dragged him away. The tiger probably yawned, wagged its tail, and growled loudly.

The same dream recurred throughout the night. Surunani had stolen a fistful of rice from the village headman's house but it was not enough for the old mother and the child. His share was watery gruel. Surunani had nothing but water. How could she assuage her hunger only by water? He saw only darkness in the bowl of watery gruel and the tiger in the dream throughout the night.

The man handed him a cup of tea and dragged him away from his dream. "Take a cup of tea my good man. Do you know what the real problem is? The times are bad. Formerly a kilogram of rice used to cost just one rupee. But now it is seven to eight rupees. So you see how difficult it is to manage. Then again, if it is the truckers on strike today, tomorrow it will the Bharat Bandh. If today the terrorists create mayhem, tomorrow it will be the Hindu-Muslim riot. Is the Malika wrong? Everybody will be equal, no differentiation among castes."

It was not in the Malika but in the Bhagabat. But he did not feel like correcting the man. He yawned. The soles of his feet were torn. It was difficult to walk. A pair of sandals made of truck tires would do good. How much would it cost? He looked at the man's pocket. Why wasn't he bringing out the money? There were a bunch of papers in his pocket. He was wearing a dirty long shirt. His Dhoti was equally as dirty, sponge chappal on his feet, spectacles on his nose. He has probably had not shaved for seven or eight days. A small garland of rudraksha was around his neck. A cigarette was between his fingers. How much would the man pay?

In these times, a man needed at least a thousand rupees per month to eat enough and live comfortably. Was I right? Besides, you needed clothes and you needed to spend on doctors. Wasn't that so? So, it would not be less than a thousand rupees.

When this scene was being enacted, Surunani would sing a prayer in Sanskrit and the children would repeat after her.

He became a bit worried. Won't the man pay? He should

say something. He did not feel like talking. Yet he spoke because if he kept silent, he might lose in the bargain. He said, "You say one thousand rupees? He will have to work hard. You see at the rate of twenty-five rupees for eight hours daily, it comes to 750 rupees a month. Then again, the child will stay there for twenty-four hours. For twenty-four hours a day should it not be 2,000 rupees a month?"

The man now looked straight at him. Probably, he thought this man was not as foolish and simple minded as he looked. He smiled and said, "Is anyone made to work for twenty-four hours? He will work in a hotel or in some household. How much work will be there you tell me? If it is a hotel, he will work for ten or twelve hours at the most. He will also get his food for free. Fish curry, Aloo Chop, Badaa and many other things. Can we eat such things in our house everyday?"

"A thousand rupees is a lot of money, my good man."

"I have to handle his mother. Let me go and tell her. If she knows, will she allow him to go?"

The man smiled crookedly and said, "Don't you know women folk are like that. For a day or two she will weep. Then everything will be alright. She will make a compromise with herself."

"It will not be less than a thousand."

"A thousand rupees will be costly for me, my man. Do you think this is a business for me? Do you think I shall get a commission out of it? No, nothing. This is service for me. You can even say service to the country. Your child will work in a hotel in Raipur. In the beginning, he will wash dishes but gradually, within a few years, he will become a cook. Then his demand will go up. Then one day he will open his own hotel. What shall I get out of it? Tell me."

Is it not pleasant to dream? Dream. His son had opened a hotel and named it: 'Adarsh Hindu Hotel.' He saw a hotel in his imagination. Chairs, tables, and even a counter. He even pasted some colored blow ups of glamorous film actresses. He even imagined the cook and the hotel boys and washing boys. But at that instant, the tiger of his dream too appeared. The tiger yawned. Its whiskers, its striped body, its round eyes, its huge mouth and sharp teeth and tongue. He suppressed all his dreams and said, "It will be not less than a thousand rupees. Do not force me, sir."

The man kept quiet for some time. Then said, "Shall I tell you what I think? I cannot pay more than five hundred. Then it is up to you."

"I cannot sell him for five hundred. You see, a great goat will cost you five hundred. It is a human child."

The man now whispered, "Quiet, quiet. What do you think of me? Am I kidnapping your child? Do you want to send me to jail? See, my man, your child and a goat are not the same. What sort of a father are you? People buy a goat to make sacrifices. I will take your child to make a man of him. A very big man. How can you compare your son with a goat?"

"Make it 750 rupees. I need the money. This year I have to buy roof tiles. Nothing less than seven-fifty."

"No, no. More than five hundred is not possible on my part. See, it is up to you."

The man got up, paid for the tea and said, "I am going. I have to go to Lakhanpur." Saying this he brought out his cycle and put his foot on the pedal, when the man called him, "Sir, wait a bit."

The man put his cycle on the stand and entering the hotel, put his hand on the man's shoulder.

●●

"I fear for the worst."

"Why fear? Are not people going daily to distant places for such work? Will your child die of hunger in the town?"

"Who will look after him if he falls ill? Who will bother if he ate or did not?"

"He will stay in a gentleman's house. Won't he get enough to eat? Does he eat delicacies in your house? He will surely get watered rice."

Surunani remained quiet for some time. Eyes brimming with tears. Her hair was not oiled nor combed. She was sitting with her head between her knees. Without lifting her head, she said, "I won't give up my child."

He was surprised at the intensity in Sueunani's voice. He could not find words to say anything. What shall he say? How could he explain the situation? Suddenly, a pure lie rusted out of his mouth. No, his voice was not grinner even for once. He was not perturbed at all. He said in a steady voice, "Now the school has driven him away. The man has said that when he goes there, the gentleman will get him admitted in a school again."

Surunani became a little bit soft perhaps. She got lost in her dream. Her son was going to school in a uniform. She was waving to him. How pedestrian was the dream! Yet how impossible for her. Why, does she not know? In spite of all her desire to get her son educated in the school, it had not been possible. It was a matter of great surprise for her.

In the middle of this rumination the tiger growled. He could see the tiger clearly in the dark. Its eyes were burning like Phosphorous and he felt the harsh rough tongue of the tiger licking his hand. Very uncomfortable. The tiger came forward and sat before him. His old mother's dead body lay near. He told the tiger, "Eat. Eat my mother's flesh. There are big bones inside, nurtured and strengthened by experience. Come, munch on it."

The tiger sniffed and turned away in disgust. It opened its mouth wide and yawned soundlessly. Now the tiger looked at him closely, came near, sniffed him and then went to Surunani wagging its tail. It licked her feet, tasting the dirt on her feet and came away. Now the tiger was in their midst inside the room. Like a domesticated animal such as cats, dogs, goats, or donkeys, he fell asleep comfortably.

●●

"Where are you?" he asked himself, because it seemed to him he was nowhere. In his life, village politics of the Panchayat had no place nor the corruption of embezzling the college fund.

He was not concerned with the latest hot news of the eldest daughter of Mr. Mishra running away with a tribal boy. He was nowhere and in nothing, not even in his dream. Now the tiger was behind him like a faithful dog. He was walking with his son, holding his hand in his. Surunani had bathed their son with a lot of care after massaging him thoroughly with mustard oil. She combed his hair, dressed him in clean pants and a shirt. And she wondered if the gentleman would give him a pair of new pants and a shirt. Surunani had controlled herself with great difficulty. While feeding him she thought their child had not yet learnt to eat by himself, how would he eat in a stranger's house? Then tears came to her eyes. Before they came out, Surunani had given the child some parting wisdom: to obey the master of the house, listen to what the mistress says, don't create any mischief, study regularly, and do household work.

The child remained silent and agreed to everything by nodding his head. The man had thought the child would cry bitterly but nothing of that sort happened. The man stopped on the road and said, "My child, I have to tell you something."

"What is it?"

"I have not told the truth to your mother."

"What truth?"

"I do not know where you are going. You may get a job in some gentleman's house or in some hotel. I am sending you with a man to Raipur."

The child remained silent for some time. Then suddenly he said, "Are you selling me off?" The man could tell pure lies to his wife but he could not tell that to the child. His voice quivered. The child's eye filled up with tears. "Are you selling me because I asked for food? No father, I won't ask for food again." The man could not control his tears. When they came out of the house, Surunani had come running after them, to tell the child one of his milk-tooth was loose and he should pull it out. Otherwise, he would have an ugly double tooth. Now he realized how intensely she loved the child.

He began to think he was probably that inhuman as he thought of himself. He felt that same affection and looked at the child. Before the child's birth Surunani had to wait for eight years. At the time of the ceremony of the child's long life, she used to be upset.

"Every mother will observe the ceremony, but I cannot," she used to lament and made everybody upset. After worshiping many gods, after much fasting, after many rituals, she got son. At that time in spite of their poverty, she refused to work in the field in the fear of a miscarriage. And for that she was scolded by her mother.

Our honorable government selected twenty-two writers to see India, fed them and took them in an aeroplane where beautiful ladies served them cold drinks and foreign chocolates. They were shown from the sky the greenery of India, the India full of mosques and temples from the Himalayas to the southern tip of Kanyakumari. Only they could not see the small black people bent with heavy physical work and their hunger, their tears, and their sweat. The writers wrote long essays about their experience. The government spent 35 lacs for the project.

The child was still afraid of the dark and wouldn't go out at night, even to urinate. He still slept holding the mother tightly. Surunani got all worked up when the child returned home after a fight with his friends.

The man became very agitated after hearing the question, "Are you selling me because I asked for food?" His whole heart shivered and he wanted to hold the child tight to his bosom. He could manage without that five hundred rupees. He would go back with the child. His face was naturally childlike and without guile. Holding him to his bosom would make his heart light. When he was a baby, the child loved to sleep with his head on his chest. Won't the house look empty without the child?

He wanted to return immediately and imagined Surunani becoming very happy upon their return. He surreptitiously took hold of the palms of the child. Well, the man may be a broker. He said he was headman of the village Katapalli. He did not know him at all. Would it be right to hand the child over to him? Would not the man break the child's hands and legs and make him beg on the streets of Raipur?

His heart began to shake violently and caught hold of his legs. Should he go back? Yes, he should go back. At this moment he saw the cycle and the rider who came to him and said, "This is the child you were talking about?"

The man seated the child on the back carrier of the cycle and paddled away. When he came, he was holding the hand of the child. While returning he was holding 500 rupees rustling in his hand. The man looked at himself absentmindedly. He had turned yellow, black stripes here and there. He looked at himself very carefully. No, it was not a dream. He had really become a tiger, exactly like the tiger in his dreams, a real true tiger.

Exactly like the dream tiger, he yawned loudly and sat in the courtyard guarding his mother and wife. He imagined Surunani and his mother had bolted the door from the inside and were shivering in fear and shock.

SOUTH-FACING HOUSE

The road to the township is something like this: first you have to get off at a certain railway station. When you come off the platform, you will see a mid-sized market. Some rickshaw pullers will rush at you. But you do not go to the town by rickshaw, because so far, no one has gone there by a rickshaw. Besides, when you know the fare they demand, you will not want to hire them anyway. If you have some luggage, you will get coolies for two or three rupees. If you have some light luggage which you can carry yourself, then you can ask passersby for direction and walk to the town. They will point out a red clay-covered road and tell you it is a short distance.

You will proceed on that road. After covering quite a distance, you will see a level-crossing. You may ask anybody there about the shortest distance to the town. They will advise you to go along the railway line in a particular direction and tell you "it's within earshot."

You will proceed along the footpath beside the railway track, leaving behind the mini market, bent accompanied by farmland, a canal, and a cremation ground. You will be thinking of another platform ahead. Don't worry. You will see the 'pits' that is, roads going down into the underground area of the colliery. There are several such pits. All the pits are numbered. You will see a colony of brick houses with asbestos roofs. That will be the township for which you are searching. You will have to walk only for about 15 minutes more. Then you will reach the township or the colony. J had arrived at the place.

The township is small, or it may be doubtful to call it a town at all. The houses stand in a line. But the distance between the lines is substantial. There are two or three cigarette shops, a few grocery stores, and a cooperative store too. There is an M.E. School and a playground. On one side there is a public health centre. There is a separate colony of houses with tiled roofs. People from nearby villages come to this health centre. There is another hospital run by the mines. Coalminers who want sick leave go there.

People of this town are strangers to laughter. Rather they frequently get angry for no reason. After seven in the evening the roads are deserted, expect for people who are either going to the mines or coming from them.

J reached such a place on a dark night. He reached there in the evening, after sunset. A little longer and it would be complete darkness. When he reached there, he felt suffocated by the pungent smell of raw coal being burnt. The smoke was coming out of houses preparing their evening meal. In such a place, neither town nor village, how and where would he spend the night?

Leaving behind rows of houses with asbestos roofs, wading through darkness and smoke, and listening to radios at full volume coming out of houses distinct out rows and film songs, J trudged ahead. No, none of the doors here would open for him. He did not have any acquaintance here in this town.

What will he do then? He wandered around for some time. When darkness thickened, he went to the market made up of a few small-tiled roof houses along the railway track. The moment he reached there, he smelled the presence of a country liquor manufacturing unit. The foul smell was unbearable. But people around him were indifferent to the odor as if their noses had lost their capacity to smell anything good or bad.

He entered a hotel and ordered a half-cup tea. The man who was sitting in front of him ordered fruit pie. The houseboy placed two glasses on the table for him, half a cup of tea and some kind of liquid for the other. J was a little surprised. Fruit here meant a liquor! Its smell indicated what kind of liquor it was. He had thoughts of fruit and fruit juice containing vitamins he could have laughed. But he realized that he was above and shelterless in this town and that it was night. He had to find a shelter, at least for a night.

He got up and went to the owner of the hotel and asked in a low voice, "Can you tell me if I can find a place somewhere to spend the night? A total room, a rented house or simply a bench? I am quite new to this town."

The man looked at him in surprise. A complete stranger? What does he expect from him? You don't know anybody here? What a strange fellow! No relations, no friends here and you have come to get a job? Are jobs fruits hanging on a tree? In this area the market is closed after seven in the evening. You cannot trust anybody here. What a menace thieves are!

J had no option but to come away. Wandering here and there, he came to a bench in an office veranda and tried to sleep by using both his hands as a pillow. He began to think.

He felt he had become a fighter. What was sorrow? Why did he fear sorrow so much? He had written stories on sorrow, on grief, on here in the moment. And yet now in this friendless town, he was quite alone, and he did not have any money. He did not know what he would do now or in the future. Yet he could sleep on an empty stomach without any feelings of sorrow. Had our capacity for experiencing feelings and moods become non-existent?

What was the comparison to give up the job in the Health Department? Or maybe, was it right? Could he become a monument by sticking to that job? In a sense it was good. There should be some adventure in life. He would certainly get some kind of job. Which pharmacist nowadays was without a job? His resignation from the Health Department job might not have been accepted as yet. He could always go back there if nothing was available here.

J woke up at the call of someone. Opening his eyes, he saw a gatekeeper asking him some questions in Bhojpuri. The man had a staff in his hand, Khaki-colored clothes, and shoes without socks. In order to assert his authority, he struck the bench with his staff twice and asked gruffly, "who are you and why are you sleeping here?"

J tried to explain to him he had come to that town to look for a job. He also tried to impress him by telling him that he had passed diploma course in pharmaceutical chemistry with distinction.

But the watchman was adamant. "What is the use of telling me these things? Have you got permission to sleep here? Show me your letter of permission. Is your permission letter signed by a manager or personnel officer? No one below them has the authority to grant permission. This is the general office. The personnel officer presides here. Even if you get permission from the Chief Engineer, that will not do."

J tried to make him understand he had come only to meet the personnel officer. Allow him to wait there until office opened in the morning.

The watchman from Bihar got angry. Striking the bench with his staff twice he said, "I won't listen to any of your explanations. First thing, if you have got the permit, show it to me and sleep here for the whole night. Second thing, if you have no permit, then get up and go with your prestige intact. Otherwise I shall drag you to the police station and lock you up. My God, where has the time gone to? Everybody is after my job."

This time J lost his patience. "What a fool you are! I have come to meet the personnel officer. How can I get a permit before I meet him?"

The watchman stuck to his guns. Thrusting his hand out, he demanded the permit. After some more bickering J had left the veranda of the personnel office. His ears became hot at this disheartening insult. He stood on the road and began to wonder where he could spend the night.

Next day at about eleven, when he reached the office, he could not see the night watchman anywhere. The office was full of petitioners. All the clerks were busy, their heads buried in files. He asked one of them about the personnel officer's chamber. The man, with his head down, did not even look up. He just rang a bell.

J stood there silently for some time. The man, after ringing the bell, went on working, as if he has no time even to lift his head. J, once again asked him about how to meet the personnel officer. The man again rang the bell without a word.

What kind of manner was this? To every question he only heard the tingling of a bell. He waited impatiently for some time more and asked again. The man cleared his throat and almost shouted, "What sort of a man are you? Can't you see, I am ringing the bell? Why are you so impatient?"

How could J know that the only way to meet the personnel officer was by ringing a bell? He felt offended but remained silent. After some time, a peon with some files came and stood before him. The man who had not lifted his head somehow sensed the presence of the peon and looking up again snarled, "Were you dead for so long? Go. Show this gentleman to Chand Saheb's room."

Last night what he had heard from the watchman about

the personnel officer's powers, he had never imagined that he would meet him so soon and so easily. Before he entered the room, he asked politely, "May I come in, sir?"

The reply floated in, "Yes, come in." J saw the man who allowed him in was of grave manner, cheroot-smoking, and dressed in a black coat and suit. Holding his application, J said humbly, "Sir, my application."

The man from behind his cheroot asked, "What? What application?"

"From a reliable source I came to know that the post of a pharmacist..." – the application containing this sentence passed from his hand to the cheroot-smoking man.

That face did not seek any answer from him. Giving a cursory look to the application containing the words 'I offer my candidature for the same,' he said, "Our hospital has a vacancy? I did not know."

J was puzzled. How could he answer that question?

The personnel officer said, "The hospital in-charge has to send a requisition to us. Only then can we appoint somebody. We have not received any requisition from them as yet."

J went on pleading for some time. But the man sitting on a revolving chair put J's application under a paper weight and said, "Sorry, I cannot help you. Only after receiving the requisition, can we consider your case. In the meantime your application will stay with me."

J was disappointed, even though he knew the job won't be his after the first approach. Why then did he feel dejected? Coming out of the office he felt in his pocket. The few coins he had would be enough for one meal. Thereafter? What would he do in this friendless place? He did not even have return fare.

J was incapable of thinking of the future. He lived from day to day. He could have one meal with the money he had but there would be nothing left for the night. Yet he entered into the hotel and had his fill. Then he lit a cigarette. After the meal, he felt drowsy and wanted badly to rest somewhere. He went in search of a resting place in the tiny market and there he met Pratima.

The same Pratima whom he had met in the ENT ward of medical college at Cuttack: white saree, injection syringe in hand, face slightly distressed but innocent looking. Face to face they now met.

"What a surprise!" Pratima rumbled. "J, you are here?"

J too asked, "Pratima, how are you here?"

He came to know Pratima had been working here as a staff nurse for the last six months at the health center on the other side of the colony near the river.

After listening to J for some time, Pratima said, "You are the same slightly deranged fellow as before. You have not changed even a little bit. How can any strong person give up a secure job so suddenly and then go about?"

J laughed.

Pratima then said, "I am staying here alone. My younger sister, of course, is with me. But she is only 12 and good for nothing. She just about managed to cook something for me. Now she is gone to our village. The Hospital has not yet provided a guarantor to me so I am staying in a rented house. Why don't you stay with me?"

J was happy. Was there any reason why he should object? After walking a distance, Pratima stood before a locally-made tile-roofed house, turned towards J and smiled. "This is my house; that is, my rented house."

A short distance away was the compound wall of the health center and a little farther, the Veden river.

At the back, the land sloped down where the miners' colony was. It was known as the 'pit.' There was a tiny market and beyond that, a green forest where in its midst, the small railway station was hidden.

Pratima unlocked the door and entered. J was following her. First there was a veranda – you could call it a drawing room or a small room. Then there was a bigger room. Then another small room like the front room, which Pratima used as her kitchen. The house was built of mud walls. At the back there was a courtyard, but it was empty.

Pratima explained, "I have not been allotted a quarter. That bloody pharmacist stays in his own house in a nearby village but he has quarters here as well and keeps them locked.

What could J say? The job he threw away had a grant for him and a brick and pucca house with two rooms with a veranda on both sides, kitchen, latrine, bathroom and courtyards in front and in back. There were also fans in the two rooms. Time had passed there quite comfortably. He would take his meals at the hotel and spend time in the evening in the club either by reading or playing cards or watching a film at the late-night show. During the day, he left the hospital in the charge of the ward boy and would go to the tea shop and read newspapers during working hours. It was quite a comfortable life. Why did he give it all up?

Pratima inquired, "Where are you posted? Why did you give up the other job so suddenly?" By that time, he had sat down on a stringed cot. He responded, "I don't know. I am searching for something, but what, I don't know. There is an emptiness in my heart and it's not filling up. Don't know if it's a disease or not."

Pratima went out of the room they were in and then said, "There is no dhoti (like a men's bathrobe) here but this is my uniform saree; I use it as my lungi. Can you use it as a dhoti?"

J, without replying, changed his and said, "I sometimes feel I have taken my life in the wrong direction. If I could go back to my past... leave it... I was talking about that emptiness in my heart."

Pratima laughed. "You're exactly the same person as before. Your lunacy came with you. During training you were absent-minded and erratic without a care for anything."

J felt hurt. What did Pratima make of his talk of emptiness and why did she make such a remark? He knew his pain was beyond Pratima's understanding. Once you recognized this pain of emptiness, you were forever caught in its coil.

Pratima reminisced, "Do you remember the training time? What a strange fellow you were. We met for the first time in the ENT ward and on the second day, you wrote me a love letter containing a proposal of marriage."

J smiled. He knew it was a kind of play, play of love. All that was gone now. He could not marry Pratima. J could not fulfill the wants of a woman who could enter into his mental world. Love did not come so suddenly in this way.

J asked, "Then how does love happen?"

Pratima suddenly became bashful. She only smiled, her head down, and then said, "Ah! You have become very naughty, J. Does love happen so quickly in this fashion? Only in the movies, perhaps."

J replied, "You mean to say love will only come as a result of following certain steps? First: acquaintance, second: friendship, third: intimacy, and fourth: love?"

Pratima teased him, "How and when did you learn so many things about love? You have probably fallen in love several times at this point, na?"

J did not reply but asked, "Why should we follow those rules? At least why should I? Why should I follow what all the others do? Why should there always be a cause and effect relationship in everything? Why should I walk down the beaten path?"

Pratima's eyes widened in surprise. She understood some of what J said but failed to understand many of the other things. She replied, "Do you mean to say that a man and woman meeting on the street can fall in love? Do you imply that there should be no morals or rules in society? In your opinion love is here today, gone, tomorrow? Is it as brittle as that?"

J was feeling tired and said, "No Pratima. I am not saying anything. Or rather I don't know what I really want to say. I have nothing to say to this world, to this society. Perhaps I had at another time but now that is all lost. Believe me, Pratima, something within my heart is missing. The space below my ribs is filled with emptiness. I don't know exactly what's missing or how I can get hold of it. I have no faith anymore in any philosophy of life, any system of values of any commitment."

Pratima brought him a glass of cold water and handing it

over to him said, "First, cool your brain. You are a memorable man and because of that, it is difficult to forget you."

Wiping away all sense of helplessness J questioned, "You remembered me Pratima?"

She replied, "That letter you wrote to me? I still have it."

J laid down on the stringed bed. This world was a vast place. There was space for everybody, somewhere somehow. J, who was driven away last night by the Bihari watchman, was now under a secure roof. While he was cooling off, Pratima said, "Wait. Let me make the bed."

The next day, he went to the hospital to inquire about his requisition. The medical officer told him they had a pharmacist post vacant and the medical officer had submitted the requisition a year ago but nobody was appointed so far. What was the need to submit a fresh requisition? He may take J's letter now and backdate it to the date of the old requisition.

He had to go to the pharmacist to get the number of the previous letter. The man he met was not young yet was a diploma holder. The pharmacist asked J, "Where did you do your diploma? At Cuttack or Burla?"

J told him he had received his diploma from SCB. That pharmacist, who had gotten his diploma from Burla Medical College, then asked him, "Why do you want to come here?"

J, a pharmacist by accident, who had given up a secure job in the Health Department, did not know. What answer could he give to such a question?

The pharmacist then said, "I served in the Health Department. And I think I committed a blunder by giving up that job. There, in spite of everything, you had some prestige. But here are these bloody labor class people who don't hesitate to misbehave with you."

J kept quiet at this point. Argue with the pharmacist? Phew, he would be tired of looking for the right words.

The pharmacist went on, "You were in a good place. See, what do people look for in a job? There should be good society around you, good schools, and a college should be near so that your children's education is not hampered. What is here? Even a high school is three miles away. As for salary, the less said the better. In the Health Department job, there was some scope for private practice as well."

J was not that worldly. Rather, he was more of a bohemian type. He was more worried about something he had lost -- that empty feeling in his heart -- than about society, school, college etc. Marriage and family had not yet even entered into his consideration.

He remained silent. After his listening to this babble of a speech, he got the number for the requisition letter and completed his business there by about eleven o'clock.

By the time he reached the rented house, Pratima was already there. Normally her lunch break was at noon but she came early for J.

"Have you taken your bath?" Pratima asked. She then suggested, "Have the water courier provide a few buckets of water for you in the morning. There is a water tap at a distance, but water is only available from five to seven in the morning. Now there will be no water there." She further suggested for him to bathe in the river for today.

J lied to her unashamedly by saying he had already taken his bath. Pratima was probably tired. Otherwise, she would have found his lie after a little proding. So without further ado, she went to the kitchen to serve.

After lunch, J lay down. Pratima sat on another cot beside him. She said, "To live all alone is painful. That too a girl . . ."

J knew the pain of loneliness. He was, in fact, tortured by it every moment of his life. So as a sign of sympathy, he extended his hand and caught hold of Pratima's. She did not try to take her hand away and said, "Do you know when I got this appointment, I came alone with only bedding and a box? Can you believe I myself searched for a house and rented this one?"

J, for the first time, began to realize the loneliness in her life.

Every moment of her life, beneath her exterior personality, she was nakedly alone as well.

Pratima continued, "You cannot imagine my suffering and agony. How difficult it is for a young girl to live alone! In the beginning, love letters used to the pushed through my door. I became mortally afraid. I have an elderly woman as a neighbor. I call her 'Mausi.' One day I told her about my problems. Her son is a nineteen-year-old boy. One night he kept guard and as soon as the man knocked at the grates of my window, he shouted at him and that fellow ran away. After that night, the fellow made himself scarce. From that day on, there have only been women here to sleep at night."

"Why didn't he come last night?" J inquired about the nineteen-year-old boy.

Pratima shyly said, "You are here. Is there any need for someone else to guard me? I have asked him not to come." Thinking of something Pratima smiled and continued, "Mausi was asking me if you are related to me. What could have I said?"

"What did you say?" J responded.

She became shy and said playfully, "You have become very naughty; you need a thrashing." What these words conveyed he was not sure but they raised a wave of desire in his heart. He realized how lonely he was! For a long time, nobody had talked to him so intimately. He was eating, drinking, sleeping and walking about like a robot. Gradually he had lost contact with all women.

J took Pratima's hand in his -- Pratima did not shy away -- and said, "Do you remember the days at Cuttack Medical College? I had proposed to you."

Pratima's face turned red. She came a little closer. J's hand went up to Pratima's head. He patted her head tenderly then asked, "You are not saying anything."

Pratima became more bashful now. "What shall I say?"

"You did not agree to my proposal?"

"If I do not agree, could I ask you to stay with me?" she replied.

Saying this, she again became bashful. She put her face on J's palm. After some time, J was sleeping on the stringed cot, face up, with Pratima sitting beside the bed on the ground, her head on J's hairy chest.

●●

Who was that fellow? What was his designation? At this time when everybody was busy, ignoring the deterring noise of the typewriters and the murmur of clerks doing their calculations, this man putting his feet up on the table was snoring loudly! On his table everything was in its proper place: blotting paper, paperweight, pen, ink, table cloth etc., even a flower vase with plastic flowers in it. But no files, no books or notepads. In spite of the heaps of files in the personnel office, so many people milling around, and the clattering of typewriters, this man was snoring away peacefully as if nobody or nothing existed.

J did not know his name but went up to him and called him rather loudly. When the man did not wake up, he slapped his hand on the table and the man woke up and looked at him. J explained to him everything in detail and asked where he could submit the requisition letter number he had brought from the hospital. The man pointed to the chamber of the personnel officer and then went back to his snoring.

The watchman of the previous night was sitting in front of the chamber. Seeing J, he got up and asked in a friendly tone, "Is your job done?"

J did not like the watchman addressing him in the second person singular at the first meeting. Even though angry, he did not say anything. Instead he asked the watchman, "Is the Personnel Officer in?"

The watchman replied, "He just went out but the manager is in. Go and meet him."

J went in and was astonished to see a middle-aged man in shorts and half-shirt sitting in front of the personnel officer's chair and smoking a bidi and reading. The man raised his head and inquired, "Yes?"

J came out as if he had received an electric shock. The watchman asked him, "What happened? You came away?"

Someone in half pants is sitting there. The watchman said indifferently, "He is sub area general manager. He is the highest officer in this mining area."

This was beyond J's imagination. The highest-ranking officer – general manager – is in half pants and smoking a bidi!

The watchman guessed J's problem. He summarized, "You are probably new to this area. Here, people have to work underground. Can they go into the pit in full pants?"

J was pleased, not at the information but the watchman's tone of respect to him.

Once again, J entered into the chamber. The Bidi smoking and half-panted general manager asked, "Yes? What is your difficulty?"

After coming out of personnel office, J wandered around the small mining area. He had not a single paisa in his pocket. A craving for cigarette smoke was torturing him. When you wander about aimlessly, you need cigarettes. But he was surprised to realize he could manage without a smoke. Nothing whatsoever was indispensable in this world. Somehow things were managed. He managed without cigarettes. He gadded about.

That day was payday. On the roadside, many temporary shops of cheap goods had come up. Snow, powder, cheap clothes, combs, etc., and vegetables; everything was available. Definitely the small temporary market must be busy with activity. Today is 'Pagar day.' These small temporary shops were no less important for the mines than the markets of Chowringhee, Connaught Place, or Piccadelhi was for us.

People were milling around everywhere. These people somehow had changed. They had become, to some extent, proud and haughty. Until a few years back, they had been meek and mild. Like ancient Greek soldiers with steel helmets, mining shoes, and dress blackened and dirty, their life was regulated by the river of the mines. Clear signs of fatigue and premature old age were visible on their faces, like the sun on the surface of a cup of tea.

Today that helpless look was replaced by a fierce fighting spirit which looked at all others distrustfully and murderously. People were on the ground in drunken stupors quarrelling without reason. J saw all these and wandered about.

When he returned in the evening to Pratima's rented quarters, she said with some agitation, "Do you know today there was a violent quarrel in the colony and s...... heads are cracked?" What J had seen was the same thing relayed to him by Pratima. She continued, "To have two in a month is dangerous. Everybody's pocket is hot with money. So, a few fights erupt. Even murders are not unheard of. Today, fifteen cases of serious injury were referred to us by the health center in the mining area. How murderously they have attacked each other!"

Pratima trembled while describing these things. Blood and gore were nothing new to a nurse. Yet her description indicated as if she saw it here for the first time.

J said, "Do you know, Pratima, why such things happen? Here is this desolate mining area where nothing happens, absolutely nothing. Only go to work, do your shift, and return home, listen to the radio at full volume, and go to sleep. Sometimes you assisted children with their homework, scold them, exercise your authority, and at night play that old game with your bodies. How long can a man go on living like this, repeating the same old routine day in and day out? Everybody here is waiting for some exciting things to happen – a war, explosion of bombs, an accident in the mines – things that would frighten them and thereby make them value life. But nothing ever happens. In order to get some impetus to love and value life, they, in the end, play this game for a few days – the game of playing with blood." He didn't know whether Pratima understood any of it.

Changing the subject, she said, "I got my salary today. Do you know we had not got our salary for the last three months? Today I got it all with arrears. I have been here only for six months. Out of three months' salary I have sent home 700 rupees. Can you believe it?"

How much had J sent home during his one-and-a-half years' service? On the contrary, he took a few months leave without salary and wandered all over Odisha. In the end, he became tired and returned to his job. Now he had resigned from that job and was here looking for another. How much had he given to his family? Thinking of this, the soil of his mind became wet with the rain of regrets.

That evening, J asked Pratima for some money. His pockets were empty. He had not even a few paisa for a cigarette. But he felt terrible asking Pratima for money. He had tried to save his pride. Finally, he said, "You must be thinking very bad of me, Pratima."

Pratima was a little surprised and asked, "Why?"

"There should be some pride of manliness in a man. A man who has no money and does not hesitate to sponge on a girl is only to be pitied or hated as a coward."

Pratima expressed her perplexity beautifully. "Fie upon you! What is this rublish you are talking about? Don't you have any claim on my money? Moreover, you have applied for the job and probably you will get it. Then you can repay me."

Absentmindedly, J said, "Who knows?"

Out of context Pratima said, "Why don't you go back to your job at the Health Department?"

J was taken back by the question. "Why? Why are you suggesting this to me?" Pratima blushed and clarified that if both of them served in the Health Department after their marriage, they could stay at one place. Otherwise, he would be stuck here in the mines and she might be transferred to Phulbani or Kalahandi. How then would they be able to manage a family?

Pratima said all this and blushed; J felt tired. At the very mention of the name of 'Health Department,' he felt sleepy. A huge office wrapped in red tape where before you open your mouth, you have to throw money. Can anyone work there with his dignity intact? he thought.

Pratima then offered another suggestion. "After you get this job, find a job for me there as well."

"Together we will make lots of money," J sarcastically suggested.

Pratima teased him, "You are marrying me for my money, is that it?"

J knew he could not marry Pratima. She wouldn't be able to adjust to his mentality in this world where money was everything and J didn't care for money. But what was the use of explaining these things to her?

Pratima stated, "I will manage the household with very little money. You will see. Even with as little as 100 rupees per month.

"We can buy a scooter very soon then," J said displaying false happiness.

Pratima shook her head and countered, "No, no, not a scooter but a motorcycle for a man as plump as you are."

"What about a sofa set?"

"Fridge too."

"A gas stove?"

Pratima reached heaven standing on J's shoulder. "But J…" Just then, a train emitting a long shrill whistle passed through his mind leaving behind in his heart its echo.

Pratima, like the humble grass on the ground, was eager to soak up the dew of happiness. But how long did this dew last?

At night after dinner, J lit up a cigarette and was about to throw away the empty packet when Pratima asked for it. J wondered what she could do with an empty cigarette packet.

But Pratima put it carefully on a shelf in a corner of the room where she had kept a few more of his empty packets then said, "When you will not be here, I shall remember you by looking at these packets. Your touch is there. By holding them, I can feel the touch of your hand."

A strange sensation of affection flowed through his heart. And of sorrow too. J had never been able to make his love a matter of emotional involvement. For him love, began and ended with the body. And yet, at this moment, he wanted to wait for love like a young man at the crossroads of adolescence and youth, tides of love flowing through his heart but without any experience and carrying on his back the weight of waiting for a suitable time. But he knew Pratima would be unable to walk in step with him intellectually and mentally. For that, a different kind of woman was needed.

Where would he get such a woman? For a long time now, he had no attachment with any girl. He had forgotten the names and addresses of his former girlfriends. This was a strange kind of helplessness for him and he was incapable of escaping its grip.

Pratima stood for a while in front of the mirror and applied a small bit of make-up. She came to the bed and instead of two separate beds she spread one single bed. Before going to bed she cautioned J, "Don't be naughty. Just sleep like a good boy!"

And just at that time, J had to remember former associate Pratap's words. Pratap had once told him Pratima was having an affair with a medical student.

He asked, "Do you know Pratap? X-ray technician Pratap? He is now at Choudwar."

Pratima replied, "How can I forget that small boy? We all called him a little boy. You know Mini? She was a nursing student in our group. She is now at Phulbani.

"I know," J replied.

"How did you know Pratap?" asked Pratima.

"I know him somehow. There are so many people in this world and you have to know some."

"Mini and I were good friends. We met at an eye camp at Keonjhar," Pratima recalled.

J said, "Pratap told me that you were in love with a student-doctor."

Pratima was a funny girl. She neither blushed nor got annoyed. Showing no such unusual reaction she simply stated, "It is a lie."

"You really did not love that student?" J prodded.

Pratima replied, "You are beating around the bush."

"Tell me the truth." J pushed further.

"What exactly did he say?" Pratima demanded.

"I told you. . . You were in love with a. . ."

"It is a lie; you are jealous," Pratima fired back.

At this response, J felt silent. In fact, Pratap had told him about Kanak, Mini, Pratima, their whole group, who loved whom. Who would marry whom – all such things. But Pratima did not show any reaction.

Then J whispered into her ear, "You never had any physical relationship will that student doctor?"

This time too Pratima did not show any sign of anger or hurt pride. She only said, "You are very suspicious, aren't you? Saying this, she held J in a tight embrace.

When their two bodies separated, J got up lit a cigarette. The lantern light had gone out. He remained sitting in the dark. He knew Pratima wasn't a virgin; he himself had freely given manhood to women. Why then worry about Pratima's virginity?

The next morning, J went into the personnel office. He ignored the man sitting on the chair with his feet up on the table in the midst of all the babble of a functioning office; ignored the clerk, face buried in the files; ignored the girl typist; ignored even the watchman. He strode confidently towards the chamber of the personnel officer and pushing the door open he entered and announced, "Sir, I have some work with you."

The Personnel Officer was reading a newspaper. He looked up and said, "Yes? Oh -- you. About that medical requisition, that I know. Have you registered yourself in the Employment Exchange of this area?"

J responded, "No. I have registered my name but not in this area. In a different employment exchange."

"You can get your name transferred to this area, you know," the Personnel Officer suggested.

J was disappointed and depressed. That was a lot of work. It would take a long time – not less than six to seven months. During that period, how would be manage without a job?

The Personnel Officer listened to his problem and then said,

"But as per the rules, local people are to be employed, that is, all those who have registered their names in the local employment exchange."

J could not find words to say anything at this point. When he was facing the sunset of his hopes, the Personnel Officer gave him hope of an early sunrise by saying, "Let me see what I can do for you."

J did not know when this vague assurance would bear fruit. But at least he knew for now he should be out of the chamber.

At night Pratima said, "Do you know? I had come to this house only a while ago. Letters soliciting love used to the pushed through my doors and windows. I was afraid even to sleep. One day in the middle of the night when I woke up, I saw a hand stretched through the window towards me. Those ventilators you now see closed were open then and a head was looking at me through them."

"Were you afraid?" J asked.

"Afraid? What do you say? Terrified, I shouted for the aunty and those bastards ran away. A single girl working and staying alone creates a difficult situation sometimes."

"Why then did you refuse my offer of love?" he asked her, his voice quivering and full of arrogance?

Pratima mused, "To tell you the truth, I was not even aware of the days at Cuttack passing so smoothly. The medical campus, nursing hostel, matinee shows in the company of friends, marketing at Mangalabag, twelve-hour shifts, all those vakul trees, corridors of the words – experience after experience. Again, all those brief relationships with patients and their relatives like those in a railway compartment, forgetting them after they are discharged. It was a well-regulated routine life without any hassles. I had never felt lonely then. Marriage or love had not entered into my consideration yet."

"When did you begin to consider it?" J teased her.

But Pratima did not care for the teasing. She said, "The day I came face to face with loneliness, I realized for the first time how difficult it is to live alone. That day, I felt the need for a partner in life."

J again fell deep into helplessness. How eagerly Pratima was waiting for him! But he knew marriage was an impossibility for him. Every day the same monotonous routine, the same routine would follow: day after day, week after week, year after year. He couldn't live such a life.

Pratima remembered, "A woman was staying in the female surgical ward of the Cuttack Medical College. She had nobody there yet she stayed on. She lived on the free meals provided there. The ward was her home. Did you ever see her?"

J replied, "Yes, the day she died. The two pieces of silver bangles she had were taken away by two sisters."

Unexpectedly, J remembered Suma. Her enchanting laughter, her way of saying 'ta, ta, bye, bye.' He said, "There is a child in the maternity ward of I.G.H., Rourkela – Seema. She is one-and-a-half years old. IGH is her father and mother, her whole world.

Once a sweeper found a newborn baby on the campus and brought it to Chief Surgeon Mrs. Bambari. From the time she was admitted to the maternity ward a few hours after her birth, she was still there. She has been given the name Seema. She had a South Indian stamp on her face. She was a beautiful child. Her laughter was marvelous. She was an object of affection for all nurses and doctors of the world. Her birthday was celebrated with cake. "Do you know anybody who will adopt that child?"

Pratima joked, "Why were you in the maternity ward? Another love letter to another sister?"

Seema was still wandering around in the corridors of J's mind. A kind of helplessness thundered below his rib cage. He said, "What really is a man, Pratima? A ready, selfish creature who throws away a child born of his own blood to the dogs and jackals? One man is a kind-hearted person who picks up an unknown child and brings it up with love and care? Why then does man sometimes become so cruel, so selfish? Pratima, I am really unable to know what man is! Is mankind so cruel? What is he? Is he an all-developing or all-renouncing creature? Is he Buddha or Hitler? If someone good or someone bad, why then does a good fellow sometimes becomes bad for another? How do you define a good man or a bad man?"

Pratima asked, "What do you think of yourself? A good man or a bad one?"

A strange question surely. "What can I say? He asked in return, "What do you think?"

Pratima remained silent for a few seconds, then said, "Previously, I did not have a favourable opinion about you. I have seen you with many different women. But what do you have that women cannot resist? I too could not resist in the end."

"What DO I have, Pratima?"

"I don't know. Perhaps your hairy chest has the promise of safety and security," she responded playfully.

J smiled. "On the contrary, I myself don't have any shelter how can I offer shelter to anyone? All my rests of shelter are broken down. You know, Pratima, I had relationships with many women. As they say, I am a characterless fellow. Why then do you trust me?

Pratima said:
"Your heart is deeper than the Ganges;
And depth of your love is hidden treasure
If one slips into that depth and later regrets
tell me, how to overcome that pain."

Now J felt something like a pigeon cooing inside his heart. He said indistinctly, "I cannot find my heart. I don't understand myself. What has happened to me, Pratima?"

She probably could not hear. J remained wallowing in his emotion for some time and then asked. "You really love me?"

At that moment he remembered Camu's Outsider. Where the main female character was asking the protagonist, 'Do you really love me?'

And J said, exactly like in the dialogue in the Outsider, "All this talk of love is meaningless. I don't understand all that rubbish written about love in the novels."

Pratima asked in a tone of doubt, "Then you won't marry me?"

"Yes, if you want," J said indifferently. Pratima could not understand him. She said wonderingly, "Yet, you don't love me."

J could not reply. What could he say? He had no faith in words now. He could convey in words what he wanted to say. This was another kind of helplessness for him.

Pratima said, "You are a strange mad-cap. I can't make heads or tails out of your words. That's probably the reason why I love you. And you will see, one day, I may hate you for the same reason."

J again remembered Camu and the Outsider. He then asked her, "Have you read Camu, Pratima?"

Pratima smiled and said, "Kanhu Charan? Yes. I have read. But then I love Bhupen Goswami's books as well. How do you like them?"

J felt depressed. He now hurriedly got up. It became impossible for him to sleep.

Pratima asked, "What happened?"

J said, "I need a smoke."

●●

A small child was walking about in the corridors of I.G.H. Suddenly it stood before him and asked, "Tell me, what is the definition of man?"

Pratima, while putting the blood pressure measuring instrument back in its place, replied, "Deeper than the depths of the Ganges is your heart."

The Bihari watchman extending his hand questioned, "Where is your permission? Show me."

Pratap was saying: in the eye camp at Kendujhar with mine
. . . .

●●

J awoke from his sleep. Pratima was sleeping beside him

disheveled. What is this trust that allows a woman to sleep with her dress disarranged? he thought. So many words, so many sentences, yet they are unable to define a man! J felt tired and trembled, racked by an inexpressible revolt within.

His thoughts continued: Man is selfish. Pratima having an affair with a medical student. Pratap standing with a waste X-ray plate. J had pissed on the facades of all establishments. What will Seema do when she grows up? Pratima is going about her job with blood-spots on her apron.

He then asked Pratima, "With so many houses to choose from, why do people prefer a south-facing house? How many get such a house? Tell me. Pratima, I am searching for a dictionary of such new words. Shall I find it, Pratima?"

"J, what do you want to say?" came her response.

His thoughts continued: Seema is wandering around, leaving blood-spots on the medical student. Why is man standing on a structure of wasted establishment? Everybody is looking for a south-facing house. Why?

I am a failure, in the midst of so many words. I don't know, who or what I am. I don't know what I want to do or what I want to say.

Pratap is wandering around Pratima's establishment; Seema in the hospital; X-ray film wasted; J standing; Pratap holding a blood splattered plate. Pratima, what is the definition of man? A man asks why people take up employment? Spots of blood, south-facing house. Seema medical, Pratap, Keonjhar, Pratima, X-ray love.

"You mean what is the meaning of words?" J responded after a time.

J carried a burden of excitement as grass carried dew. With clenched teeth he said, "I want to destroy all words of this world. I want to create new words. Show me the way."

Pratima turned in her sleep. She was only half awake. Wriggling in bed she asked him, "What happened?"

J said enthusiastically, "I have to create many new words, Pratima. Existing words have become old and useless."

Pratima's eyes were again closing. Probably she did not hear. She said in a sleepy voice, "Go to sleep. Sunrise is still far away."

J had never thought such an anxiety and worry would be solved so soon. That morning, he went to the personnel office, without looking at the man dozing in his chair with his feet up on the table; or at the clerks hunched over their thick files; or at the peon in front of the office. Without permission, he had gone into the office and called the personnel officer who was writing something.

He looked up, saw him and smiled light like the warm sun in a cold morning spread around his face. He said, "There you are. Here, take your appointment letter. When will you join?"

He brought out a piece of paper from a file and handed it over saying, "Take it to the clerk. He will put a number and you can take it after signing the peon book."

J trembled, but in happiness or fear? When he took the piece of paper, he felt as if all his energies had evaporated. He didn't have the strength even to hold on to the paper as if it would fly out of his hand. Why was his hand shaking so abnormally?

Somehow, he managed to control himself and came out. Ahead was the residential colony of the mines. People with helmets on their heads were going to and fro. Everyone was surely depressed. Nobody expected anything from anyone else. Yet everybody was restless by this monotonous routine.

This road, these houses – everything was plunged into a fog of pain. He felt all those are very old, very old, very familiar and very boring. He would have to forget the vast world outside and one day imprisoned in this limited world, he with just vanish? Would he make himself a presence here and willingly accept self-banishment?

The more he thought about it, the more he felt terrified. He wanted some proof of his existence! But how? If he stayed here, after some days, he would forget his own appearance. Even standing before a mirror he would fail to recognize himself. Is this what he wanted? Rather he would prefer to go back to his old job in the Health Department and back to his old town. If nothing else, he could be in touch with the outside world there. That was not possible here. There was no way he could escape from this narrow, limited world.

He came back to Pratima's quarters. She would be in the hospital now. Should he go to her and talk her? "Pratima, I came here to win. But what kind of victory? I did not ask for such a victory. Please forgive me, Pratima," he might say.

He would tell her, "Pratima, nobody is indispensable in this world. Without me you can go on living just as you are living without that medical student. I feel sorry for you. Still I cannot stay here because I want ground, soil where I can experience the salty taste of my blood and the taste of iron in the water. This land sent me back with empty hands. Forgive me, Pratima." No, he could not say all these things to her. Better not to see her.

When he came, he had not brought anything with him. Now while leaving, he had given a lot to Pratima. Many memories, some deception. Deception? J shivered. In his imagination he said to her, "Have you understood, Pratima, that we did not really love each other. We both wanted to avoid loneliness and hence surrendered each to the other. Mind is far above this body. When a body gets dirty, it can be cleared. But when mind gets dirty it cannot be washed. Believe me, my mind has no dirt in it."

He got up and saw the empty cigarette packets lovingly arranged on the shelf. He went nearer and affectionately touched them. In his mind he said to Pratima, "Like these empty packets, I too shall become a memory to you. You will keep them all arranged in the compartments of your heart. Do you know this is the most valuable thing one can have? If you got me within these your walls, very soon you would begin to feel that you had lost me somewhere in some corner of this house. Much better you keep me imprisoned in your memory and occasionally revisit me. Bid me adieu, Part time."

Reaching the railway station, he found that the second bell for a coming train had already rung. He did not ask whether it was an up or down train or where it would go. He asked for no details. He brought out a handful of coins from his pocket and thrust his hand through the looking window.

The booking clerk asked, "Which station?"

Which station would he go to? Where could he get the proof of his existence? Standing on what ground would he be able to get the warm salty taste of his blood?

J said, "Give me a ticket to a station which this much money can buy."

The booking clerk looked at him in surprise. As the third bell rang, he quickly gathered the money and gave him a ticket.

When he entered the platform with the ticket, the train was already standing. He entered into the compartment in front of him and sitting down on a bench, took a breath of relief. And just at that moment why did he have to remember Pratima?

Now it was eleven o'clock. Pratima would not have come back from the hospital. After returning would she able to realize J has taken leave of her for all times to come? Perhaps she would wait for him to take lunch together. Then wait and wait. J would never come back. Would Pratima wait for him forever? That happens in stories and novels. Who waits for anyone forever? Have you seen a mirror? Life is like the mirror? A mirror does not preserve the shadow of anyone. When you go away, the shadow is removed from the mirror.

The train whistled. People standing on the platform get into it. The guard waved his gun flag from the last compartment. The train slowly moved forward. J got up, went to the door, and waved his hand. But there was no one there to see him off. Whom did he wave to?

J went on waving until the platform vanished from his sight. He was waving and whispering inaudibly, "Bye, Good bye."

■

A FLIGHT STALLED
IN HIS TRACKS

"Giving all possessed
to strangers
Shiva the God
ran away naked."
(An Odia proverb)

Divyendu came to visit Arunav at the same time as crown-sized paperback edition books by Shivananda arrived. Inside in English, there was Shivananda's philosophy of life, yoga, sadhana, Samadhi, and days to realize god-titled practical lessons in yoga.

And Divyendu, a five-feet-four-inch tall young and robust man, very dark complexioned with high-powered spectacles who was preparing to appear at the cost accountancy (CA) exam privately. He prepared his own food in a cooker; an ordinary sorrow-ridden young man. In fact, he was so ordinary, in this age and time, he cut his hair very short and applied a lot of oil to it and wore fourteen-inch bell bottom pants. At that time, he was employed as an accounting clerk.

Arunav was someone whose designation was 'technical advisor' and who had long, stylish hair; wore bell bottom pants; and was a bohemian type, wandering around a lot without caring where he worked. So much so, he did not think about his future; stayed as a paying guest; did not bother to argue about God's existence; and most important of all, did not follow any order or discipline in his life; and who wrote poems and stories. Arunav thought outsiders didn't understand him and yet were attracted towards him because of something in his personality. But that something gradually vanished like the laws of static electricity -- as they came closer, they were not only turned away but sometimes become outright enemies. Hence, he tried to remain alone as long as possible, through this loneliness was something like the blood and marrow in his body; something as natural as the breath he took. And he sometimes wondered if he could ever live without this loneliness.

Shivananda's books came on the same day to Arunav as Divyendu. At first, Arunav was a little hesitant about what to do with both as they did not exactly fit into his lifestyle. He did not have any interest in the practice of yoga, but that day, after listening to a two-hour long speech on the need for the existence of a supreme being, if not God, he had come away somewhat influenced by these ideas.

Meanwhile, Divyendu had come to him and told him his CA exam was ahead and he was unable to rent a good house and since the company he worked for had not provided any financial aid to him, could he come and stay with him? Although Arunav was of two minds about his being able to adjust with anyone, he could not say no to Divyendu. So the next day, Divyendu arrived at his place with all his belongings: cot, table, bedding, box, cooking utensils, books, notebooks, paper and pen, etc. While Shivananda's book occupied Arunav's mind, Divyendu occupied Arunav's whole house.

Arunav's quarters were on the top floor of a flat which was a covetable possession for the middle-class people of Rourkela. It was a one-bedroom house. A bedroom and another room which could be designated as a drawing room without any objection. There was a passage-like space which could not be called a dining hall but could accommodate a dining table. There was also a latrine and kitchen and fans in the rooms. People here called it a B.R quarters.

Upon arriving at Arunav's flat, Divyendu first removed Arunav's cot and put it in the drawing room; he put his own cot in the Arunav's bedroom. After putting his table, which measured three-and-a-half feet by two-and-a-half feet, along with two chairs, there was no space for another cot. So, he told Arunav somewhat in the tone of giving an order he hoped Arunav would have no problem sleeping in the drawing room. Arunav was a little bit hurt but he was of such a temperament that he was unable to protest face-to-face so, he did not say anything to Divyendu. And Divyendu went further. He pushed into a corner of the shelf all of Arunav's books, magazines, manuscripts of his stories, and arranged all his own books on costing at the front part of the shelf. He then removed Arunav's clothes from the wall and hung them on the drawing room wall. Still Arunav could not say anything but realized henceforth, he would be a refugee in his own home.

Arunav's troubles started that very night because of the mosquitoes and heat. The only ceiling fan was in the bedroom. In the drawing room, he could not hang the mosquito net because of the heat and without it, the mosquitoes had a field day. Divyendu had, of course, told him to sleep on the floor in the bedroom and for that purpose, had pushed the table and chair into a corner and spread the mattress on the floor. But Arunav refused this generous offer, as it would mean that Divyendu would sleep on the cot and he, Arunav, would sleep on the floor. Divyendu's sandals would be there as well. Besides his mattress and all this in his own house, he was being treated like a servant. Yet Divyendu did all this without any qualms as if Arunav had no reason to feel insulted or offended.

Arunav carried his cot and bedsheet and Shivananda's book along with his distress, anger, hurt pride and feelings to the roof and slept there. It was a long-standing habit with him to read himself to sleep. As there was no light on the roof, he forced himself to sleep but could not. Then he went down to his room and brought a candle and lit it, keeping it carefully near the bed so the mosquito net wouldn't catch pyre. He tried to read Shivananda's book, sitting inside the net, although he felt sorry at the insulting behavior of Divyendu. He came across a poem of Shivananda which went like this:

"Adopt, Adjust, Accommodate,
Bear insult, Bear injury,
This is highest sadhana."

These few words so influenced him he not only recited them again and again but also prepared himself mentally to put them into practice. If nothing else, Shivananda's book taught him discipline and Divyendu's presence brought cleanliness to the house. Prior to Divyendu's arrival, Arunav had no such discipline. Eating, sleeping, bathing, and even writing his stories were all done at no fixed time. Even making his bed every day or sweeping his rooms, those daily chores he neglected or left undone out of boredom.

The same Arunav now got up at four in the morning and without brushing his teeth or taking his bath but only washing his face, sat down to practice concentration but his mind was like a disobedient child after school started, running here and there. As a result, Arunav consoled himself by thinking he would have to keep up the practice and gradually his mind would be under his control.

●●

Divyendu's touch made the house look clean and fresh. Books were not pell-mell; cigarette butts were not found on the floor; spider webs and soot were removed from the corner of the roof. Even the fan looked bright and new and the house was swept clean twice a day. But even after all this, Arunav felt something somewhere was broken down irretrievably and he had become a refugee in his own home. He would console himself by reciting Sivananda's couplet.

"Adopt, adjust, accommodate
Bear insult, bear injury,
This is the highest sadhana."

From that moment on, Arunav tried to adjust, never objected to Divyendu's selfish behavior, went on sleeping as before -- sometimes on the roof, sometimes in the drawing room in the heat. Divyendu, on the other hand, had become completely indifferent to all these sufferings of Arunav, as if they were not unbearable on his part.

Arunav would sit at Divyendu's table on one side to read and write; Divyendu would sit on the other side. He was very disciplined. At eleven, he would switch off the light and go to sleep because light hurt his eyes while sleeping and he couldn't sleep unless it was dark. Arunav had not such fixed time-table. Sometimes he would fall asleep at eight; sometimes while writing a story if the spirit of creativity moved him, the whole night would pass without a wink of sleep.

One day, both of them were sitting at the table reading. It was eleven o'clock at night. A mood for writing a story had come upon Arunav while Divyendu was yawning audibly. After some hesitation, Divyendu got up, switched off the light, went inside his mosquito net, and asked Arunav to go and read in the drawing room as he would be unable to sleep if the light fell on his eyes.

He said these words in the dark as if he was afraid to make eye-contact with Arunav. And Arunav was so mild in nature, he could not get up and switch on the light and tell Divyendu it was his house and things would run according to the way he, Arunav, wanted. He would go on reading as long as he wanted or sit wherever he wanted and however long he wanted.

But he did not say a word, although he was suffering within, he wouldn't say anything to Divyendu about it, even though it was insulting and humiliating. Yet he got up and took his papers with him, sat down on his cot in the drawing room, and tried to continue with his story. But his mood had spoiled. He then went to the roof, walked back and forth, and declared war against Divyendu and fretted and fumed. And all this while, Divyendu was sound asleep on his bed downstairs in Arunav's own room.

Divyendu could not but notice Arunav's effort at Yoga practice. When Arunav was trying to concentrate his mind, just then, Divyendu would cross the room in front of him and Arunav would feel unease at the sound of his feet as if the practice of yoga was something childish or an outright sin. Moreover, even if Divyendu's presence disturbed his mind, he could not tell Divyendu not to disturb him. Just as Shivandu's book told him: for practice of yoga, a separate room was preferable; it should not be used for other purposes. Its doors and windows should remain closed. It is better to have a photograph of your god or goddess, or Jesus on the cross, or Mother Mary, or the Kaba Mosque. A blanket needed to be sat on when doing yoga practice. The room should be purified by burning incense sticks at all times. Care should be taken to see the room was not cluttered with unnecessary items. The aim should be to see when you entered the room, you should have an atmosphere of purity. If a separate room was not available, one should have a corner fenced off by cloth screens to make a prayer room.

Listening to the book, Arunav's mind was filled with regrets. If Divyendu were not there, it was not difficult for him to get a room for himself. But now it was not possible to get a room all to himself. Remembering this, he felt Divyendu had become a burden on him and he had surrendered the keys of his freedom to him.

If this whole affair stopped at that, it would not have mattered. But one day, Divyendu even dared to make fun of his practice of yoga. Even after Arunav explained to him the benefits of Pranayam and Samadhi, Divyendu began calling him jokingly 'Mr. Shivananda.'

The next morning when Arunav sat down in the lotus position to concentrate on the Agnya Chakra, the place between the eyebrows, and tried to meditate on the formless form of Lord Jagannath, his mind, wearing the garb of Divyendu's taunts, started wandering here and there and someone seemed to be whispering in his ears, 'Mr. Shivananda, Mr. Shivananda.' And the echo of that whisper pervaded his whole consciousness.

He stopped his meditation and got up. Shivananda's book told him. He had insulted only your body, mind, and your small ego; you are not that. But he had not insulted your real ego, because he is a part of your real ego. By insulting your small ego, he has, in fact, helped you in separating yourself from your small ego.

After consulting Shivananda's book and thinking long and deep about it, he decided to remain silent hence forward and wouldn't talk much with Divyendu.

Shivananda's book told him by disregarding or rejecting realities of this world, man increased the power of his consciousness. Hunger and thirst control your mind. If you could keep your desires, impulses, and feelings under your control, you would see your mental strength had increased. This mental strength was necessary for your (sadhana) practice of Yoga. According to the instructions in Shivananda's book, Arunav removed all his bed linens, except a thin piece of cloth matting, and put them all in a bed holder and put it under his cot. That very day, Divyendu brought home a new soft but thick mattress and chattered about its good qualities for half an hour. At the time of sweeping the room, Divyendu brought out the bed holder from under the cot and threw it somewhat arguably and carelessly on the shelf below the ventilator in the bedroom.

Throwing the bed holder in this way may be an insignificant

matter but it hurt Arunav deeply, as if Divyendu had thrown a big piece of stone at is chest disdainfully. Sleeping on his cloth mattress, Arunav began to think whether he should get angry with Divyandu. Yes, why shouldn't he? He should and must. No, probably not, at least for the sake of Sadhana.

Swimming between doubt and hesitation between yes and no, he opened Shivanandia's book and recited, "adapt, adjust, accommodate, bear insult, been injury, this is highest sadhana."

But many small things irritated Arunav. For example, Divyendu's habit of reading audibly although he kept the radio on while writing stories and he had written quite a few good stories while listening to Hindi Film songs. Divyandu had monopolized his hangers and Arunav had no option but to hang his clothes on a nylon cord or on nails stuck into the wall. Divyandu even used his soap case. As a result, he has to keep his wet soap in the wrapper. When he returned at night at about eleven o'clock, after carousing with friends, Divyendu got up to open the door but with impatience at Arunav. All these things had made Arunav feel sorry for himself. He had felt hurt but every time, Sivanada's book had advised him to be egoless, selfless, and to rise above mundane affairs and be calm and quiet in all situations.

That day, of course, when he returned home at his usual time of eleven o'clock and found the door locked with a different lock, other than the one he had given to Divyandu, Sivananda's book had no effect on him. Divyendu had gone out locking the door with a different lock without bothering to tell Arunav.

Arunav came down step by step and wandered along the street. After a very long time, he came up again and found the house still locked. This going up and coming down a few times made him very irritated and burning with anger. He decided that enough was enough and he would ask Divendu, when he got back, to vacate his quarters. But Divyendu did not return and being tired of loitering on the road, he finally knocked at the door of his neighbor, Mr. Nayar, at midnight and after explaining the situation, asked him to allow him to go up to the roof where he would wait. They had a common roof and each house had a staircase to go up.

Mr. Nayar obliged him and allowed him to go up. How long could he wait! He took off his shirt and sleeping on the roof, went on thinking, all the while cursing Divyendu, counting the stars in the sky, tolerating mosquito bites, and feeling helpless, and fell asleep.

In the morning he faced Divyendu, full of anger, and when he asked about the different lock, Divyendu replied nonchalantly he had some urgent work at the station and as he was in a hurry and could not find the right lock, he locked the door with his own.

But Arunav was such that face-to-face with Divyendu, he could neither scold him, nor ask him to vacate his quarters, nor throw away his things. He said nothing; rather, he could not. He could only open Sivananda's book and recite: "adjust, adapt, accommodate…"

Another day, as was his practice, he returned at eleven o'clock and knocked, and Divyendu, after a while, opened the door. As soon as he entered into the drawing room, Divyansh whispered into Arunav's ears, as if he is imparting some deep secret, "Arunav, my girlfriend is in my room. She will stay here tonight. Spend the night on the roof, please."

Girlfriend or a prostitute? What sort of girlfriend was she in this city of Rourkela who could spend the night with a boy? Divyendu's bedroom door was only half closed. It was dark inside. The sound of the fan whishing was audible. Arunav could not think what he should do now. He took off his shirt and pants and put on his night dress. Divyendu remained standing. He went to the bathroom and washed himself. Divyendu still remained standing. He dried himself with a towel and without uttering a word went up to the roof with his mosquito net, his mattress and a bedsheet, and a pillow. He could hear the closing of the door with a thud and the sound of locking from inside.

Dibyendu's way of closing the door made him suddenly

burn with anger. What should he do now? Should he wake up the people in other flats and till them that Divyendu had brought a prostitute into his home?

At first, he thought like that but he controlled himself. Sleeping on the roof inside his mosquito net, he felt helpless. He was a refugee in his own home and whereas Divyendu was gambling with a prostitute in his bedroom, how long could he go on carrying this dust of insult and disregard in every drop of his blood? How long? No, he had to protest. He was not a coward to go on tolerating every torture of Divyendu heaped on him! He was a man and he had some individual preferences. Why should he give up all that?

No. He will knock on the closed door and call up Divyendu and as soon as the door was opened, he would throw him out with his things along with the prostitute. And he would tell him sympathetically, "I am the owner of this flat, understand? I allowed you to stay here without any rent out of kindness. You should have understood that much."

Arunav got up, angry and advanced towards the door. On the point of knocking at the door, he felt his legs had gone numb. He had lost all his courage. He didn't even have strength to lift his hand. His feet were as if melting away, becoming as shapeless and liquid as water. A kind of coldness was creeping up towards his knees. Sivananda's book was left behind in his room. It could have given him some advice, some consolation, at least some way to deal with the situation. He tried to utter the words with difficulty, "Sivananda, what shall I do?"

But no words came out. He remained standing like that, with great difficulty. His feet were melting away like butter.

RAYAGADA – RAYAGADA

Hearing my son was reading at Rayagada, all my acquaintances were somewhat surprised and asked in incredulity, "Rayagada! In Rayagada?" As if Rayagada was not in Odisha, not on this earth, nowhere in this universe.

From the Rayagada railway station going towards Nakua hill, my son stood still looking at it. "Father, do you see that hill? It seems as if a man is sleeping contently there."

I too saw that and was surprised, "Yes, so it looks!"

At a short distance from MIITS Engineering College, the Naxals had landmined a stretch of the road. It was evening. A police vehicle was blown up; my son showed me the spot. Towards Bhubaneswar from Rayagada, a few kilometers from the J.K Paper Mill colony, a little after Amalapet, the road was broken up, tar and all. That day I felt happy. In the middle of the road was an ash-colored hole – a sign of the revolution. Rebellion, then, was still alive!

It was 1969 or 1970, I don't remember exactly. From the border check post of Jamshola Ghat, at a distance of eight to ten kilometers from there lied Bahadogoda Township. National Highways 6 and 36 met there. From there, I got into a bus for Ranchi. Ghatshila, Tata, Chandil and two or three more bus stops – I don't remember the names now -- then Ranchi. The bus left in the morning and reached Ranchi by about four or five o'clock in the afternoon. It was a bus belonging to the Bihar Road Transport Corporation. The conductor told to me ten rupees without a ticket but eighteen rupees with a ticket. He first taught me the nationalization of corruption. Inside that bus, I read from a newspaper the police had arrested in Jadugoda jungle a group of Bengali Naxalites and an English woman with them. Jadugoda jungle was in between Ghatshila and Tata. How thrilled I was! Revolution, then, was not far away?

I was under the impression the fat black man sitting at the counter of the familier hotel was an Odian. Later on, I came to know that he was from Telugu. He asked me smilingly, "Visiting your son, sir?"

"No. This time I have some other business."

"What other business?" he questioned.

I was a bit unprepared for such a question. How can I tell him why I came there? Could I tell him? Finally, I told him, "A friend lives here. I have come to meet him."

Known hotel, familiar people, and familiar smell. Even the room was familiar, the strange musty smell of the room, the bed and the sheets – everything had a familiar, strange obscene feeling of a layer of dirt.

The hotel boy changed the sheets and switched on the TV.

He had to fetch the remote control from the next room. He saw the pelmet of the window was broken. The screen was hanging somehow and may fall down any moment.

After arranging my things, I took out the letter from the suitcase. His letter.

His handwriting was round shaped. Very beautiful. Why then, did he not continue his study? He wrote poems but did not go to college. Could have sat at the cash box in his father's saw mill. But leaving everything behind, why did he roam in the jungle?

I opened the letter. He had written, "My dear friend."

Was I ever dear to him? Far back in the seventies we met twice or thrice. In the intervening years I had received only two letters from him. This was his second letter. Between these two letters, there was a gap of probably twenty years. With such little contact, had I really become dear to him?

We first became acquainted at the Cuttack convention of the S.F.I. Then, he had stayed with me in my hostel room for two or three days and took his meals in the hostel mess. He used to vanish during the day and come back at night to sleep. It was a pleasure to listen to his conversation. He used to say then he was immersed in Naxalite activity and he had gone underground.

In his absence, I once opened his bag. There were some books by Gananath Patra, some poems, a few copies of Samukshya and Frontier magazine, a Khurdha-made bathing towel, a brush and paste. Nothing else. Not even an extra pair of pants and shirt. He was not poor; his father was a man of property. This I came to know two years after. We met once at Anugul bus stand. I was on my way to Belpahad to see my elder brother. At about one or two o'clock in the morning in front of the hotel Neel Kamal, we met. He embraced me with joy. I noticed he had not changed at all. Unshaven beard. He was smoking a lot of Charminar cigarettes then. He caught hold of me and said, "I won't let you go. Let's go to Athamallik."

Almost forcibly, he quarreled with the bus conductor to get

back the money I had paid for my fair. Then we came to Athamallik by a truck which had gone to Talcher from Athamallik carrying a load of timber. There I saw in Athamallik, his father's large saw mill. His father had made a pile of money from the timber business in such a small place like Athamallik? He had a three-story building. He put me up in a wooden structure at one end of the saw mill. In the midst of the saw dust, the noise of the saw mill running and general commotion, he read me his poems. I saw two things there for the first time: The Red Book of Chairman Mao and the special technique used in using saw dust to fuel a handmade oven. The heat generated by such a process was quite intense.

"Dear friend." He had written, "Come to Rayagada at least once. I shall take you to the villages on the other side of Nakua hill. There you will see what real hunger is, what real poverty is. Come once. I will show you what exploitation means. I will show you how the old mother of Nadu Mangeji Kandha died of starvation, when bananas were selling at 10 for five rupees. The Government said she died due to lack of nutritious food. You come, I will show you another Odisha from Bhubaneswar. It is the Odisha of Rayagada. You come. I am confident after you return from here your thoughts and ideas, your style of writing stories, your attitude and outlook everything will undergo a significant change. You will then see the whole of Odisha is a Rayagada and it is shivering in a high fever. You will see a salon on the Hati Pathar road in Rayagada. Its name is Vizag salon. Emanuel Majhi works there. Tell him my name and he will bring you to me."

He addressed me as "Dear friend" in the second letter as he did in the first.

When the first letter reached me, at that time, use of a telephone was not so widespread. People used to wait for the postman. The first letter was of that period. He ended the letter with "Yours Bipin."

Who is this Bipin? Do I know anyone by that name? I could not recollect immediately. I looked at the address: Bipin Nayak,

Manikeswari Saw Mill, Athamallik. Then I remembered the sawdust oven, the Red Book of Mao Tse Tung, the sound of the saw mill running and in the midst of all, the recitation of poetry. It appeared to a real close. A dear friend indeed.

"Dear Friend." In the first letter he had written: "Although my postal address is the saw mill, you will not find me there. If you come, I would be at a distance of 25 kilometers from Athamallik. In the jungle, by the side of a stream with flat stones all around, I have built a house all by myself. This place does not bear any name. I do not know on what latitude or longitude it stands. But then sometimes I feel this earth is completely new and is created for me. It is as if we are the first human beings here.

No electricity here, no phone lines, nor any path for the postman's cycle. Here I have set up my home. My wife Surubali is here with me. In her womb is growing a new life created by my own seminal fluid. If it is a son, I shall name him Stalin; if a daughter, Gargi.

For my house I have dug out the clay, Surubali prepared the mud dough. We did not know the technique of building a house. In the process we came to acquire all the mechanical knowledge associated with it. I felt man is the source of all strength. If we had not built the house, this great dignity of a human being would not have been revealed to me.

I called up a few men only for thatching the house. Otherwise everything else Surubali and I have done. Even the twig-woven doors. You won't understand the tremendous pleasure we derived from building our house with our own hands. In every dust particle of this house, we mixed our own sweat, our memories, and our labor. Sleeping on a bare mat on the floor of this house is more satisfying than a comfortable bed can give.

You may think I am exaggerating like poets but that life can be lived like a poem, I realized only when I came to this jungle. For the first time I realized what hunger is, or fear, or attachment, or love. For the first time I realized how beautiful life is and how necessary it is and how small is the real claims of life.

Now Surubali and I have reclaimed a piece of farmland. Next year I shall have a pair of bullocks and start cultivating. We both will work in the field. I will plough the land and she will take out the weeds. I will raise the seedlings and she will carry them to the threshing yard. I will harvest them and she will blow away the tar.

Now we are the primal male and female. We work throughout the day, prepare the field, put up bonds, and turn up the soil. In the evening Surubali cooks rice. When it boils, she sits there with her cheeks on her knees tending to the pyre. I sit at a distance and write poems in the light of a kerosene lamp. I read the poems to her. It is surprising that she understands poetry. She expresses her opinion freely regarding the quality of the poems. Nature has taught her the secrets of poetry."

Hati Pathar Road, Vizag Salon, Emanuel Majhi and riding piggyback on a motorcycle through the lush green fields extending to the horizon, hills, chimneys of distant factories, trucks plastered over with Telgu letters jumping down the road towards an isolated village behind Nakua hill. What was the name of the village?

At one end of the village was an asbestos-roofed schoolhouse. The Headmaster's office occupied one end of the building. Then came classrooms from first to fifth standard. Then, I had met him in an empty room. Mustache and beard were turning grey but the hair on the head had not yet turned white. A lungi and a sleeveless vest made him look like a Telgu schoolmaster from a distance.

On the blackboard, a worked-out sum still remained. Nobody thought of wiping it clean with a duster. There was a stringed cot covered with a handmade quilt and bedsheet. In a corner, some clothes were hanging on a rope. Below it, an earthen pot on sand with an earthen plate cover and a glass for drinking water. Beside the wall was a wooden crate on which were kept some old books and papers. A framed photograph of himself with an Adivasi girl in their youth, a nose-ring and a flower-tattoo on her fore head was noticeable. In the other corner, were a kerosene stove, a small cooking pot, and a blackened curry pot. A few plates and cups upturned on the ground.

The room was so full of dust you feel it when you walked. I looked around. There was an old torn broom behind the door. A mat on the floor on it with some papers, a book, two pens, spectacles. He was probably sitting there writing. He had just gotten up. Seeing me he was surprised, "You have come! Unbelievable. I never thought you would come. Come, come, come inside."

Nearly thirty years ago, we had become acquainted. He wrote to me after reading one of my stories. Then one day, all of a sudden, he arrived at Ravenshaw. After two- or three-days' uneasy stay, he went away. The second time we met at Anugul, Athamallik. After a long gap, this was our third meeting. Where was Surubali? Her child about to be born? What happened to the mud hut made by his own hand in the jungle of Athamalik, his farm land? Many things were unknown to me. There was a lot to ask.

"Everything got lost. That's how it happens. That is Nature's law," he said. Caressing his unshaven beard twice or thrice he said this. I marked his fingernails were uncut and blackened. But his eyes were wide and impressive. I could not fathom whether they expressed indifference or apathy. There was no smile, rather, a sort of gravity pervaded his face. Probably, he was somewhat desert-minded.

He had said, "Life is like this. It flows like a spring. It does not stop. Goes on changing its surrounding. To stop is to die. If the water of the spring stops flowing, will it remain a spring? No, it stagnates and becomes home to insects, amoeba and moss."

I could not get any information about Surubali from him. What story was hidden behind his leaving the mud hut in the jungle and coming to Rayagada did not become clear. I said, "Bipin, leave aside these ramblings. Tell me what really happened."

"Surubali left me", he said and added, "Of course she cannot be blamed for leaving me like this. She was a girl of the jungle. I am a child of the town. I wanted to live the life of a townsman in the midst of the jungle. There was a difference of culture between us. We both had to adjust. Then one day we decided no, it is better to go our separate ways than to continue to live in this uneasy adjustment."

These were all unsolved arithmetic problems for me beyond my thought and comprehension. Seeing the puzzlement in my eyes he had said, "You don't believe me, no? Then listen again. I don't know if I can explain anything better."

He continued, "Surubali needs the gruel of the kernel of the seeds of mango and tamarind to feel satisfied. I need a plate of hot rice. In summer, plenty of Mahul, Mango, and blackberry made her forget the taste of hot rice. Red ants and their eggs in the hollow of a tree, mahul flower, young bamboo soot and eel fish in the stream – everywhere Nature has stored food for Surubali. But for me an oven and hot rice. I needed too a pinch of salt, two green chilies, a drop of mustard oil. Between us these things – an oven, green chilies, mustard oil, and salt created the gap.

I shall not blame Surubali. She was like that. I wanted to be like her but could not. Mine was the inability to be her fit partner. One day I told her, go, fly away. I release you from your cage. That day the cheerfulness in her eyes was something to be seen. She was like a deer free of her enclosure. Her going away enchanted me. How beautiful freedom is I realized that day. While going away, she did not forget to take Stalin with her. How far motherhood is animal-like. She gave an eyewitness proof of that."

"But Rayagada? Why Rayagada? How Rayagada?" I questioned.

At my question he looked at me with his wide eyes. He said, "Have you read the novel Shiba Bhai by Gopi Mohanty? It was written fifty years back."

I replied, "I have not read Gopinath Mohanty so far. That is my shame."

He continued, "From Muniguda station to Kalyanpur station. Nowadays Kalyanpur is known as Kesingpur. Nearly is J. K. Paper

Mill. Leave it aside. Between these two stations is the Niyamgiri mountain range. It stretches for 36 miles and achieves a height of 5,000 feet. Below this mountain range flows the river Nagaabali. In that mountain range lived the Dongria Kandha.

Dongria Kandha – the males are nearly six feet tall and quite strong physically. If you had come here fifty years back, you would have seen the Dongria Kandha with two or three nose-rings, ear-rings, a strong but small rod of brass or bell-metal tucked into the bun of hair, on the head, glass beads round the neck, a thick metal wrist band and a sharp curved knife hanging from the loin cloth round his waist.

Today if you come to Rayagada you will be surprised to see the Dongria Kandha. They do not have that outfit now. Now they wear pants and shirts. No nose-rings anymore. They have come down from above the mountains to the valley of the Nagabali and have set up homes beside the river. Fifty years ago, for fear of the tiger, the Dongria Kandha were urinating inside the huts at night. Now there are no tigers in the jungle around Rayagada. The houses of Dongria Kandha no more look strange. They are provided homes under Indira Awas Yojana. In our school, many children of Dongria Kandhas are reading."

He got up to prepare tea. He poured water into the saucepan for three cups of tea and he said as if he was offering an apology, "Nagaraju has come. He has gone to bring some Sambar meat. It is good thing that you have come. I shall feed you Sambar meat. But fresh meat is not available here. The Dongria Kandhas keep dried meat. You can say decomposed meat full of bacteria. It smells but very tasty. You can eat and know."

Bipin's description made feel like vomiting. I had goose bumps. Bipin said this was the difference between our cultures. "You don't feel like vomiting when you eat dried fish," he had remarked.

Nagaraju came. By this time his tea in the cup was cold. He had a thick moustache, dark complexion. He looked nervous. Seeing me, he felt afraid and forgot to say, "Laal Salaam."

Bipin introduced us. I was a comrade and wrote stories.

Was I comrade? Bipin's comrade? I remembered our college life of the seventies Cuttack Convention of SFI. In front of Ravenshaw College on the dais of martyr Pradipta's memorial service, a speech delivered by Nabakrushna Choudhury. There had been the strange excitement of writing slogans on walls during the night.

Still then was I a comrade? Ever? Had not Bipin read any of my writings? How does he find signs of revolution in my stories? How?

Bipin introduced us. "This is Nagaraju. Naxal worker. My favorite comrade. Today we shall visit his home. Shan't we?" Nagaraju said he could not procure Sambar meat. Before he entered the village, people said the police were looking for him and advised him to flee.

Bipin seemed not to care. He said, he read in the paper how Sabyasachi Panda hoodwinked the police and attended his mother's funeral rites at Nayagarh and came back.

Nagaraju hailed from ViJanagaram. From his college days, he was interested in Marxism. First, he became a member of SFI. Then a Naxalite. Candra Babu Naidu's police once arrested him. While being taken to the court he escaped from the clutch of the police. On the run since then, he had not visited his home.

The Police were on the lookout for him. What if they arrived right now? My middle-class mind was apprehensive. My family would be ruined. In the seventies, someone had called me to participate in an action.

At that time, I could not take up the step. My middle-class family, middle-class hopes and desires, and its achievements and failures kept me back. Those who called me to join the action did not go to the jungle of Gunpur or Rayagada. Simply, a kind of fear kept me away from the revolution.

Today in the afternoon of life, it was as if Nagaraju was calling me again to join an action. Even now those things were still possible for me.

Nagaraju swallowed his tea in one gulp and said, "I am going. The police may reach here any moment. They have quite a few detectives in the village."

Bipin seemed not to care for his words and said, "Sit down for a little while. We shall chit chat. Tell me how your family is?"

Bipin continued to me, "This Nagaraju is very dear to me. Do you know why? His present and my past are not different."

Nagaraju smiled and said, "I am teaching Telugu to Swetalana. She now can read and write.

Do you know who Swetalana is? Nagaraju's wife? She is a Kandha girl of this village. Now they have built a house in the jungle and live there. That's why Nagaraju reminds me of my past. I had not changed Surubali's name; I could not change Surubali. But Nagaraju is careful. He has changed the name of the Kandha girl to Swetalana."

I remembered the first letter of Bipin. 'For my house I dug up the earth, Surubali prepared the clay. Now we are preparing a field. Next year I shall buy a pair of bullocks and start cultivating the land. We are now the primal man and woman. We work at the land throughout the day. In the evening Surubali cooks. When rice starts boiling, Surubali keeps her cheek resting on her knees and keeps looking at the fire. I sit at a distance and write poetry in the light of a kerosene lamp.'

Nagaraju went away making me uncomfortable. Bipin and I were silent. On the blackboard, an unsolved arithmetical problem was displayed. Nobody felt the necessity of wiping it away. After a long silence, Bipin sighed deeply and said, "You are a story writer. You can say. Tell me why this happens. In the unending flow of time, one story repeats itself again and again. Why? Or how?"

I did not have any answer except a long sigh.

A FIGHT WITH MEPHISTOPHELES

Bhubaneswar, I shall be killing you within a few days. From Chandarasekharpur (Patia) to Bhimatangi, from Badagarh to Khandagiri, your 999 temples and 99,999 clerks, your uncountable prostitutes, unrecognizable housewives, unlovable leaders, intolerable news reports, beyond the reach five-star hotels and flights. I shall kill within a few days all the buildings of BDA and all the houses of Housing Board. I shall kill the artificial houses of Konark, the Pagoda of Dhauligiri. I shall kill the six-foot tall arrogant girl in a yellow salwar suit who waits for an unknown train at Bhubaneswar railway station every day at nine o'clock and will show you what true love is!

What else could I do? Was it possible to shake off sick words from the stale advertisements hanging on your body? If women did not wear sarees, what would the students and teachers of the Art colleges do? Would they continue their study of beauty in nude studies? Every winter Navy Balls, on every 31st December, open invitations by bars during the poetry recitations on the roadside. Every morning on January 1st money was counted in Malisahi to see how much income which prostitute made the previous night. All the problems started when women began wearing sarees. Anarchism succeeded everywhere after legislative assemblies were formed. Tell me Bhubaneswar, from where shall I shake off the words? You know Bhubaneswar, how insignificant you are in the whole world, how valueless, how ugly, yet you are the lord of the universe.

A sixteen-year-old Draupadi's hand raised in supplication was running on the street of the capital, crying "Save me, save me." Following her were Duryodhana and Duhshasana. Like the royal court of the Kauravas, the people of the capital were interested but indifferent, self-centered but alive and awake. All the shops were closed for her. The darwan at the factory gate threw her out. The garage owner did not even allow her inside. "This is your private affair, do it on the road. Why are you involving us?" the owner had said. Not a single piece of stone fell off the Lingaraj temple at the piteous cry of the girl. The bells of the Pagoda did not ring out. Just at that time, the ever-awake watchman of democracy went for his lunch. The girl was still crying out, "Save me, save me." Duryodhana, Duhshashana at one stroke tore away her skirt and blouse. A butcher ran toward the police station. Was he Shree Krishna? Nobody remembered him.

Nobody remembered his heroic act because they don't have egos, no self-prestige, no hatred, no shame, no history, no tradition, no myth, no past. They don't bring in the names of Arjun, Yashoda, Radha, Sophocles, and Cleopatra at every turn. They had forgotten their memory since long ago. They didn't have 21st century, no world war, no world peace, nor any claim on the metals of Antarctica. Since long ago, they have forgotten their coming down and have lost their calendar. They don't go to the market to buy a book of poems or to the street with placards, or to the bathing ghat with newspapers. They don't have watches. They had forgotten time.

Before the killing, our cadres were distributing our manifesto secretly. The hit list was being prepared: the Daya River would be poisoned. Poisonous gas would be spread in the air through the chimneys of the factories near Mancheswar. Oxygen would be sucked away from the atmosphere. Every sapling being planted on the road side would be eaten up by cows. At midnight, a siren would go off. The fish plate from the railway line would be removed. An overdose of Morphine will be injected into the sleep of the householders. Very soon I shall kill you Bhubaneswar – before a beautiful dawn broke.

Keeping the museum at its back, what sort of justice were the courts busy dispensing? Like a naughty boy, BJB was winking. Pissing or masturbating? Even at the very back of the judge's chair nazeers, clerks, lawyers and their clerks, all ask for bribes. "Buy justice, buy justice." Stamp paper cost three rupees, but the vendor sold it at five rupees. Was justice so cheap? Even cheaper than rice, dal, oil? The head clerk in the office of the sub-registrar had made it a rule: 1,020 rupees for the Government and 1,005 rupees for our office expenses. Nothing was shameful near the courts. Neither masturbation nor rape nor robbery. Injustice and ill judgment were always safe behind the safety bolts of the courts.

Behind everyone else, someone was running. Who was he? Everyone looked at the nearest fellow in suspicion. Like the hunter's dog, someone or something may come stealthily and attack. Palpitations of everybody's hearts had become faster. Everybody wanted to keep his family safe by hiding them behind their door screens. Overcoat for the winter, raincoat for the rain, cooler for the summer. Even when stars began to shine in the sky, everybody looked suspiciously at everybody else. Who knew? Meteors may begin to fall or an out-of-orbit satellite may fall?

Who knew if the lover coming to kiss the beloved may have tiger claws hidden in his hand?

Still, long lines had formed before banks for BDA plots. Ten to five officegoers told their wives to reduce their household expenses because a house was more necessary than calories. Ministers, MLAs (politicians), lecturers (professors), film actors; everybody was rushing about.

Danei who came from Brahmagiri to pull a rickshaw here was now lying in fever. In a hut behind Bapuji Nagar, he kept on looking at the Konark Hotel throughout the year with his bloodless eyes. Rainwater leaked through the roof while white ants had eaten away the bamboo twigs inside the mud wall. His hand-made quilt was full of bugs. Allotting plots by BDA continued. Long lines were formed before banks. The peon of the municipality was going around with the notice regarding demolition of unauthorized slums.

What audacity on everybody's part to surpass everybody else. All wanted to prove how capable they were. For this narration of life, everybody had come out to participate wearing sporting banyans. Whereas, the moment you plucked a flower, it turned to charcoal in your hands. Everybody you met was a stranger. Nobody laughing intimately told you, "For a long time, you have forgotten your appearance. My dear man, are you overwhelmed with sorrow?"

A dead body was lying on the parade ground. Nobody saw it – people taking a shortcut from PMG square to the bus stand, intellectuals bored with the highbrow speeches in the Suchana Bhawan, clerks taking French leave from the secretariat, girls of the NCC riding past early in the morning, young men and women looking for love in the dark night, nobody saw the corpse. Nor did the people crowded round private buses, nor the enchanted, blind elderly man of the family looking for a history book for class seven, nor the governor accepting the salute, nor the ministers holding up the country -- nobody saw it. The corpse lay there since a long time, year after year. It lay there but never decomposed;

the putrid flesh didn't fall off. The atmosphere was not poisoned by the foul smell. From ministers to beggars, from a chaste woman to a prostitute, from a writer to the clerk of a lawyer, everybody was buying ground nut packets without a care to throw away like wrappers in the parade ground. I shall build a mausoleum there. I shall write in the epitaph, 'Do not disturb. Truth is lying here peacefully.'

Last night, somebody knocked at the neighbor's door. "Sahoo Babu, Sahoo Babu, open the door please, your mother is serious ill." There was no Sahoo Babu in the neighborhood. Yet the man went on shouting, "Sahoo Babu, Sahoo Babu." The whole colony trembled at his call. A temporary lockout was declared at the factory made by the silence of the night. "Your mother is seriously ill. She is in hospital. Open the door." The man went on knocking, knocking, knocking but no Sahoo Babu stayed in the neighboring quarters. In the dark room, Mohanty Babu, Ray Babu, Subudhi Babu, and Pati Babu, all rummaged in the darkness and found Carpose tablets, gulped them down and went to sleep. The man went on throughout the night calling, "Sahoo Babu, Sahoo Babu, open the door."

I have spread the mines. All arrangements for the conspiracy were complete. I had formed my formidable army of terrorists. I had set up my secret wireless network; also procured hand-held rocket launchers, and hand-made pistols and guns. In the jungles of Chandaka, I had set up my secret armory and arms manufacturing factory, and our secret radio station. I was waiting for the action to begin. Within a few days, I shall kill you, Bhubaneswar.

"Shall I do it; can I do it, Bhubaneswar? Every flower you stretch your hand to turns into charcoal, Bhubaneswar. Every man I meet is a stranger. Bhubaneswar, you are the universe, you are life, you are the existence of my tiredness. How far I run away from you, always, everywhere, every moment you are around me, Bhubaneswar. All the charcoal in my fist, all the men laughing the laughter of strangers – all are you. Not being able to make anything of themselves but sleeping the sleep of self-satisfaction enchanted by the world – all these people are you, Bhubaneswar.

I am tired, exhausted. See, I discard my armour. Take my hands, my legs, my torso around my head. I retire from this marathon race. Take my sporting banyan. Take my shoes, handkerchief, and the nobility of chewing gum. I know the charcoal in my fist will never turn into flowers. No one will ever hold up a mirror to me. I know, Bhubaneswar, after I kill you, another Bhubaneswar will spring up in every corner.

This is a declaration of defeat until the date which guerilla war has not been defeated. In the middle of the war, Che Guevera gets lost, the half-naked Fakir is shot dead. In the middle of the war, Bhishma gives up arms. And all victims and defeats are like the climax in stories and novels.

Am I a cynic? Do I not know that the tender morning is playing in the courtyard of the nursery school? Have I forgotten the butcher Sri Krishna who ran to the police station to save the sixteen-year-old Draupadi? Yet I am tired, exhausted. I have come out of the marathon race. All my manifestos I leave behind in the courtyard of the nursery school. I have decided to accept defeat even before the battle is halfway through. This is my cowardice, my unreasonable fear; this is my helplessness, my unhappy defeat.

Now your conspiracy against me has begun, Bhubaneswar. Now you are putting mines. You have prepared your plan of action. On your hit-list my name stands at the top, Bhubaneswar. I am ready for your ugly laughter in the sodium light. I am prepared for the excited shouting of your office-going crowd at ten o' clock. I am ready for your ego. I am ready, I am ready. Even now my fist holds only charcoal. Even now I have lost my own mirror in the unfamiliar laughter surrounding me. I am ready for you, Bhubaneswar. Where shall you put up my gibbet?"

ALL THAT GLITTERS

One would not normally imagine a mere round earring could hold the ingredients of so many stories. But as it happened, it was only a small round earring which had become the main subject of discussion in the office. And everyone was coming out with a story from the treasures of their own experiences.

Arunabh opened his palm. On his way to the office, he had picked up a round earring lying on the road, glittering in the sunshine. He knew it must be a girl's, fallen off at some careless moment.

He had shown the ring to everyone in the office. Haripada Babu, an L.D. Clerk (lower division office assistant), who had seen it first, had commented, "This is brass. Who would throw away a gold ornament?"

"Why?" Arunabh responded. "This is a child's and could have fallen off her ears."

"Maybe be it did fall off," replied Haripada, "But this is not gold."

Arunabh further responded. "This is brass. Otherwise it would not have been so hard."

Mohanty Babu, U.D.C. (upper division office assistant) rubbed the ring first on his palm and then on the floor and said, "There might be some gold in it. Why don't you show it to a goldsmith? One can never be sure about these things. I had found a golden sovereign (British coin) once. Everyone said it was brass, but the jeweler had found it to be made of pure gold."

Mahendra Babu, Dealing Assistant, looked at the ring from all sides and said, "It would be glittering if it were gold but where is the shine on this one?"

The Head Assistant who was closely scrutinizing the ring, offered, "What gold have you seen? Have you seen Sambalpur gold? Looks like brass but a hundred percent gold. This must be Sambalpur gold." Then he made as if weighing the ring on his palm and said, "At least six grams. Might get about 30 rupees. But then again, it is not a good thing to find gold. According to shastras, losing gold and finding gold are both bad omens."

The Head Assistant's words gave fright to Arunabh who was listening to their discussions. In some dark recess of his mind, an ominous bird started circling and a dark cloud cast its shadow over his face. Arunabh shivered a little.

Haripada Babu said, "Nonsense. This is pure superstition. Imagine saying that in this age of science."

The Head Assistant was about to say something in rebuttal but Mohanty Babu, U.D.C., said, "I don't understand why you always come across as a know-it-all. I personally know how ominous getting gold could be. The year I got the gold sovereign, my father died. Our house was gutted. We lost everything that year. Otherwise, I would have been running my business like a prince, not having to push my pen in this office."

At this, Arunabh's fright increased. His left eye had been fluttering, which was a sure sign of some bad luck to follow. On the blank sheets of his mind, he started typing out all possible bad news and shivered as he tried to erase them out. He felt as if he was in a leaky boat lost in a sea of ill luck.

The L.D. Clerk showed Arunabh a way out. "Go to the goldsmith," he told him, "if it is gold, sell it and make an offering of five rupees or so in the temple. You can't throw away 30 rupees."

All except Haripada agreed with the suggestion. But Arunabh was still apprehensive as he held the ring tightly in his palm.

When the office closed at noon for the lunch break. Arunabh came out and showed the ring to the owner of the pawn shop. The shopkeeper gave Arunabh a look of surprise and then rubbed the ring on his palm. He said, "No, sir. It may be rolled gold or brass but never pure gold. Can't you see the dark marks it has made on my palm?"

Not gold? Arunabh felt disappointed. If it were gold, he would have at least gotten something out of it. So, what would he do with a brass ring?

While eating his lunch, Arunabh showed the ring to the restaurant owner. "This is a gold ring," the man confidently stated, "Pure Sambalpur gold." Arunabh again saw a flicker of hope. The man added, "Can't you see the Sambalpur workmanship in the ring? The trouble about this type of gold is that it doesn't glitter."

Serenades of joy played in Arunabh's heart. Birds of hope fluttered in the skies of his mind. But as he was closing his eyes to savor the happiness, the restaurant owner said, "To find gold is not good. They say it's bound to bring bad luck."

The music stopped. The birds got lost. A dark cloud of fear now floated past Arunabh's face. To find gold was not good. What might it bring? Death? Accident? Fire? Robbers?

Arunabh saw a funeral procession. Whose dead body was it accompanying? He closed his eyes. It was his father's face. A gold ring circled his neck. Oh. God!

A demon was beating an old woman. Robbers were ransacking the house. The old woman was lying senseless with a broken skull; her face had turned grotesque. Upon regaining consciousness, she was crying, "My son! Where is my son?"

Arunabh was being thrown out of the car in an accident. His hand had been severed. Blood splattered. Arunabh was rolling on the ground.

Arunabh left the table shivering. His lunch half-eaten, he went to the wash basin. The restaurant owner called out from the counter, "Leave the ring with me. I know a jeweler. I'll have it checked."

Was he trying to trick him? Arunabh wondered. Suspicious, he said, "No, I am going to the jeweler now myself."

The man sounded disappointed when he said, "All right." Arunabh wondered and held fast to the ring wrapped in paper, in his palm.

It was blazing hot outside currently. When he came out from the shade of the shop where he was buying cigarettes, he knew it would be impossible to go out in the hot sun. He was accustomed to taking a nap in the afternoon. But today he called a rickshaw and asked him to take him to a jeweler.

The first jewelry shop was closed. In the second shop, there was only a child sitting who told him he knew nothing about gold. In the third shop, the goldsmith said, "Sir, a child was born today in my house. I cannot touch gold until I take a bath."

The rickshaw puller, fed up now, said, "There is only one other shop a mile away. But that too is bound to be closed too as it is that time of the day. Better you come in the evening."

How could the rickshaw puller understand Arunabh's anxiety? "Let's do that shop also," Arunabh told him. But the rickshaw puller had the last word; he would take three rupees.

Even that shop was closed. Returning home, Arunabh

decided he would try again in the evening. He had to know if the ring was made of gold and if so, how much it would get if sold.

But it was possible the jeweler might cheat him. No, he must bring the Head Assistant along if it was found to be gold. If he got 30 rupees, he would give offerings of five rupees in the Shave temple. Or maybe he would make offerings of two rupees each in the Shiva and the Vishnu temples and a rupee worth in the Lakshmi temple.

What if there was a mishap? Arunabh's left eye had been fluttering for the last three days, surely a bad omen. He had not received any letters from home. Was someone ill in the family? Arunabh worried about his thatched house in the village for fire was a common hazard during the summer.

Back in his room, he changed into a lungi (garment worn by both women and men usually from the waist down). While going to hang his trousers, he wanted to take out the change from their pockets. And then he got a shock. There was no round earring. He rummaged through both the pockets, pulled the shirt and trousers inside out. But there was no sign of the round earring.

He searched the floor, the mattress. The round earring seemed to have vanished into thin air. Where could it have fallen? In the rickshaw? On the road? In the jewelry shop? What was the number of the rickshaw? Would he be able to recognize the rickshaw puller?

Arunabh dressed again and came out. It was unbearably hot outside. Where would he go? How would he retrieve the ring? Which road would he take?

He leaned against the door frame. It was not good to lose gold nor to find gold. He did not even know if it was brass or gold. But it was true it had been a burden on him and it was now gone. He felt a certain vacuum, as if there was something missing. How strange his heart should feel vacant for such a small thing. Arunabh kept standing there, leaning against the door frame.

RATS

Debarchan and Susmita had been waiting for good news for the last few days. They looked forward to being smothered by it. So, they went on waiting until they felt the hour was at hand. They knew their prolonged wait would come to an end shortly and they would be transformed. They would become a different type altogether, metamorphosizing into something much better and beautiful. And so, they started to mould themselves suitably in anticipation of their new type. Their surroundings should be recast, they felt; their house should be renovated. A proper beautification of the house should commence at once, as an overture to the metamorphosis.

Debarchan paced the floor of the living-room, lost in thought, his eyes scanning its interior. What should he do so the room would look unusual? What changes should be made to make it look better? He looked around when he saw the beautiful curtains on the window facing east. The ikat design on it had lost its splendor, and badly so, at the crucial point in the cleft. The window curtains on the west were, however, in good shape so he took off the curtains from there and exchanged them with the curtains hung on the window facing east. And while putting them back, he took care to hide the cleft of the curtain behind an edge of the almirah. Debarchan now turned his eyes to the walls. The ravages of time were clearly imprinted on them in a uniquely self-styled way. A patch on the south side, its white point having peeled off, revealed the plaster underneath.

He called Susmita and pointed out the patch on the wall to her. Susmita listened to everything attentively and then racked her brain. Really, what should they do about it? Debarchan joined in her inquiry. What should they do indeed? Then Susmita saw a way out.

From the bedroom, she fetched the calendar with blow ups of the Konark wheel on it advertising for the Konark Cement Company. She hung it on the wall in such a way that it hid the lime-bleached patch on the wall. A smile lit up Susmita's face as he marked her success; a smile escaped Debarchan's too. Their smiles compounded; smiles blending pride and joy.

On the north wall, Susmita discovered a patch on it slightly above the ground which had shed its pigment like the other wall. What could be done about it? She brought it to Debarchan's attention and they both pondered over it. This time, the answer struck Debarchan. He shifted the convertible sofa lying on the eastern side of the room and placed it northwards. The single sofa lying south was hauled to the west. Now the room seemed to wear an unusual mask. It looked as if the house was not theirs but belonged to someone else!

But no, they did not stop there. They went on to change and improve the interior decorations. They finished the drawing room and took up the bedroom. After the bedroom, the kitchen and then, the dining area. Debarchan did not go to office that day as the entire day was spent beautifying his house. He was so engrossed in the job that he completely lost track of time. He hadn't eaten breakfast when he should have, and he didn't shave nor bathe in time either. Instead, he shaved during the lunch hour and bathed when he should have taken a nap. He ate lunch during the post lunch hour when he usually went back to the office. After lunch, he returned to his redesign tasks in the house. A feeling of ecstasy welled up inside him: the house wore a new garb. Was it their own house or someone else's?

Simple joys and small pleasures, but enough to send them into raptures. But as they were cheerily chatting about it Susmita, bumped into something. It gave her the shock of her life. Open-mouthed and fearful, Susmita was on the verge of tears. She revealed it to Debarchan. Debarchan too, was surprised, his shock complementing his misery.

The fact was this: on the east floor, where their Bombay patterned cot was placed, they found many holes. God! How many holes there were! And how big they were! How had they come to be there? Had they been made by rats? Which one had been scooped out first? How many rats had been working on them? And which rat had taken the lead? No one could answer these questions now. The leader, who had dug the first hole was perhaps oblivious to it now. Still, holes lay strewn across the floor. Holes for sure; holes being hollowed out every now and then.

In the middle of the night, the sound reached Susmita. She heard it. Debarchan heard it too. They both cocked their ears in the direction of the sound for some time. Then Debarchan tried to hush her to sleep saying, "Phew! It's probably nothing."

"But you can hear the sound," Susmita questioned.

"Yes, that's the sound," Debarchan replied.

"It is coming from inside the house."

"Not exactly, from outside."

"But I feel It's from inside the house; from near our heads."

"Might be coming from the ceiling too."

"Really?"

"Might be coming from the other room too."

"Really?"

Susmita did not speak another word and turning her back to Debarchan, went off to sleep. Debarchan too remained silent and turned over to go to sleep, but they could hardly get to sleep even as the night pushed on. Debarchan wondered if Susmita really fell asleep? Did she really fall asleep so fast as that as they were barely halfway through their conversation? She should not have; she should have kept awake awhile more. She should have stroked him once more, as usual. She could not fall asleep just like that. Every night she would reach out to Debarchan, her hand lying on him. She would stroke him for a long time and would caress him until sleep gradually came to her.

Was she therefore asleep now? Debarchan wanted to make sure and put his hand on her when the sound was heard even more violently. Susmita began to shiver. She was awake now. She turned, faced Debarchan, her eyes filled with fear and then asked Debarchan, "Do you hear me?"

"Yes," Debarchan replied.

"Shouldn't you see to it?"

"What is there to see?"

"The sound. Where does it come from?"

"And at this hour? We should have done something then . . ."

"Yes, something for sure but what?"

"Then you ask me to get up?"

"Mmm-Hmm."

"Then you ask me to put on the lights?"

"Please do."

"You ask me to switch on the courtyard lights?"

"Should I unlatch the door now and call the neighbors, now, at this hour of night?"

"Go to sleep. It's late already."

"I can't sleep with all this racket, man."

But hardly a second passed when Susmita quietly fell asleep. So did Debarchan. Both were lost in deep slumber 'til early in the morning. But when they awoke, they heard the sounds again, the same sound which like a bad stink was flowing through the silence of the room. Debarchan looked at Susmita awestruck; Susmita was terrified too. She gaped at Debarchan. Debarchan was feeling miserable.

Debarchan questioned her, "Do you hear that? It's the same sound as last night."

She replied, "Didn't I ask you to find out about it last night itself? You never listened."

"Do you make out anything? The sound comes from inside the house."

"But from where, exactly?"

"From under the cot, towards our heads. Shouldn't you get a stick or something just in case?"

"I will but I really wonder how we slept through the night without giving a damn about the noise?"

Susmita now responded angrily. "You rest all the while on that cot and go on babbling now like this?"

She got up as she said this and straightened her saree. Lifting her suitcase from the top of the big wardrobe in front of the cot, she put it on the floor. Then kneeling, she put her ear to the leathery wall of the suitcase.

Debarchan was still in bed. He asked, "What is in there inside that box?"

"The sound I feel it is coming from here," said Susmita. She unlocked the lid of the suitcase and opened it; a rat leaped out. Susmita was scared and let go of the lid. She recoiled from the scene, overcome by fear and anxiety.

Debarchan stood up, went near the suitcase, and picked up the lid. My Gosh! he exclaimed. The suitcase had become infested with rats! Small ones. Red ones. Gray ones. Black ones.

Rats colored absolutely black, grey, and red in all manner of shades and hues.

An entire dominion of rats ruled from within the suitcase. The sun rose the moment the suitcase was opened. An empire of tiny rats woke up to this morning, bathed in sunlight. Empires whirled within empires queuing rats. Who would stand where? Beside whom? Who would lead, leaving footprints behind? It was such a problem; the domain was the inside of a suitcase.

Gusts of wind rattled the rat empire. Still, they needed more. They seemed to cry out into the vacuum, "Give us air, pure air. We need air for us to walk, to be able to kiss. We will die without air. We will be suffocated."

Expensive clothes lay piled in that suitcase: Debarchan's shirts and pants, Susmita's sarees. Their radio license was there. Their love letters too. Rats screamed in triumph over their tiny relatives. And two tinier black globules of their excrements presented themselves leaving a rotten stench.

Debarchan overturned the suitcase causing an earthquake in the rat empire. A small rat tumbled down, its limbs thrust upwards, and moaned. A big rat rushed towards it. And a meek rat dismounted from a heavy rat's back. Rats small and big, strong and meek. Yet another rat crashed. As though in a game of hide and seek, one rat was foolishly looking for another. It scurried along and made off somewhere. Gasps. Tears brushed off on a crooked glass slab. Shot plopped down the nostrils. Moans faded out.

"Where did they go?" Debarchan asked.

"To the hill," Susmita responded.

"To the hill? What hill?"

"Where does it go from the hill?"

"To the hill's regime."

"Where is the hill's regime?"

"There, where the sun shines brightest."

Parched, the sobs of the rats reached the hilltops. They formed clouds there; the clouds formed rain. The rain hastened towards the surface of the earth. The rats skated in the slush and then skipped into their holes. What happened after that?

Susmita swept the rest of the floor. Debarchan emptied out the suitcase. Susmita then turned to take stock of her sarees. "Look here. My Devnagari (pink) saree is reduced to rags by the rats. Your terry woollen bellbottoms are in tatters. My Benarasi silk saree is all torn and my chiffon Georgette is in shreds. See the radio license; all torn. Our precious love letters, all gone!"

With this, Susmita broke down. She sank into her bed and wept bitterly. Then her tears gave way to helpless sniffing and sobbing.

Debarchan comforted her. "Don't lose heart, dear. Sarees, shirts, the radio license, our love letters are all trivial things. I will get them for you again. But don't cry. My heart breaks when you cry."

Susmita stopped whimpering. She wiped her eyes, blew her nose, and washed her face. She gathered up the torn clothes which had been strewn on the floor -- her sarees, Debarchan's trousers -- and folded them properly. She put together the ripped radio license. But what could she do with completely torn love letters? Not even a sentence was left intact. She threw the scraps into the hearth.

Debarchan, sitting cross-legged, observed it all. He did not utter a syllable but looked on, like a saint. He too felt like breaking down but decided not to yield to his impulses.

●●

Days rolled by. Debarchan went to his office. While working there, he heard a sound like: 'krr krr.' At times, the sound swelled from a murmur into a racket in front of him, at his back, above his head, and under his feet. This 'krr krr' sound sang out from under Debarchan's chair, inside the drawer, within the files lying on the table. He opened the drawer, shuffled the files, and kicked the table.

The rat empire pervaded inside the drawer, within the files, and under the table. Their slimy coats dyed in grey, black, and red. An entire team of rats was doing acrobatics: somersaulting, chartering, and scampering about. They stood up on their hind limbs with folded palms. They giggled, their whiskers quivering as they did so. They got scared for nothing, ran away and collided with each other. The rat on the red rat's back; the red rat on top of the grey rat. A rat flipped on the floor; another shouted at him: 'krr krr krr' —a cacophony of rats could be heard. One nibbled at the other. Another rubbed its feet against another's, tickled him, clambered up his back, tickled him again. Yes, he did it, really. So what? Everyone did the same. Everyone did it before falling asleep. Everyone did it as they tittle-tattled. But did they do it as they ran? Or did they stand a while as they did it? They tickled others and got titillated in turn. Tickled ... teasing sensations. Krr krrs aroused the rat empire and then retired it into uncharted recesses.

Debarchan's workstation at the office was a mess: yellowing files pulled apart by rats; filth and stink; a mutilated chair, table and drawer, and above all, a krr krr sounding through the air echoing within itself. Debarchan finally broke down. Pained, he paced about and then left the office for home.

Susmita did not wail anymore. Rather, she was in a cheerful mood as she welcomed him. She grinned widely and said, "Hey, you know what happened today?"

A withdrawn Debarchan asked her, "What's that?"

"Your books," she replied.

"Books? My books?"

"Were bitten by the rats" Susmita roared with laughter. "Hey, look here."

"What's that?"

"The radio," she replied.

"What happened to the radio?"

'The rats have destroyed it." Susmita crackled like mad, totally different, as it were. "You hear me?"

"Now, what's next?"

"Your bedspread."

"That too?" he queried.

"Yes, that too has been minced, man! What fun!" Susmita gave out peals of laughter, as if nothing had gone wrong and it was all so enjoyable.

Debarchan was much too hurt to react. The rats were causing one loss after another but look at the way Susmita was responding! Her giggles grew louder and louder 'til Debarchan snapped at her: "Stop it, Susmita. Please stop your goddam giggles." But at this, Susmita became sillier and seemed to have turned into a laughing machine. She clutched at her belly and howled, "That rat, there."

Susmita rolled on the bed in terrifying bouts of laughter. Water welled lip in Debarchan's eyes. He couldn't make out if this was happening spontaneously or whether something had got into his eyes!

●●

Now this occurred every day; at the office and at home. Debarchan felt he was changing; he was changing into an abnormal being. His daily schedule, he felt, was all messed up. He slept at odd hours, ate when he ought to be shaving, and took post-lunch naps when he should have been at his office.

That day when Debarchan returned from his office, no one was at home. Susmita had gone out leaving the house open. He snuck in. Everything was topsy-turvy: the sofas in the drawing room were displaced; the lime-peeled patch on the wall revealed the ugly cement underneath; the slit on the window screen which had been hidden scrupulously behind the almirah had opened out and the rats had made the house a thoroughfare. Unwashed clothes, books, an ink-pot, utensils still containing leftover food were scattered on the floor. A stink pervaded the air. Where had Susmita gone leaving the house in such a mess?

Debarchan made his way into the bedroom and threw himself on the bed. The rats did not care for him anymore: a rat hopped into his lap; another on to his head. Rats bit his toe. A rat fell off his leg while attempting to climb it.

Debarchan felt he was going through a veritable hell. Never before had he experienced such sinister times. He had been waiting for a time that would fetch him good tidings. It never came. And since it never came, Debarchan could now foresee the sorry times ahead. They had begun, he knew and a lot more of the same were yet to come.

Debarchan brooded over his fate. And then he came across a teacup in the bedroom with a little tea left in it. A lone teacup, used. Susmita did not take tea. Then, had someone come? He found burnt-out cigarette butts all over the floor. Susmita did not smoke; neither did Debarchan. Who had then smoked cigarettes here? Who had come to his house? And to his bedroom? Where did Susmita abscond? For God's sake, who had occupied the bedroom in his absence and smoked there? Who had half drunk the tea and sullied it? And where on earth was Susmita?

Krr krr krr ... the clatter echoed again, this time it became an uproar; krr krr stirring within itself. Debarchan realized he had still a lot more to lose while Susmita was determined to go ahead with her menacing laughter.

Debarchan's days passed; so did Susmita's. He went to work every day as usual. Almost daily, while combing her hair, Susmita would be lost in her thoughts. Debarchan returned home late almost every day. Susmita invariably went to bed without food. And the rats further exercised their sovereignty in the house, slowly, rhythmically, day after day. Dirt filled the air. The digestive waste of the rats was everywhere. The sofa, bedcover, door curtains; everything had been torn to pieces by them.

But the way Susmita laughed with such gay abandon as the rats wrought havoc before their eyes presented problems for Debarchan.

Once Debarchan tried to articulate his feelings to Susmita. "My sadness is great Susmita. I am feeling terribly depressed these days."

Susmita surprised him with her reply. "I too am sad Debarchan. I too am feeling depressed and dejected."

Debarchan poured out, "And you add to my misery too, Sus."

Susmita repeated like a parrot. "And you add to my misery too, Deb."

The anger within stifled Debarchan into a silence. He sat there still, with a heavy heart for a long time. Why couldn't she sympathize with him? And then he spoke out. "Amid life's ocean of sorrows. I had sought a little happiness from you, Susmita!"

Susmita, without a moment's delay, crooned into his ears, "Amid the uncertainties of life, I too was certain of your love, Debarchan."

Debarchan wanted to squabble with Susmita. His heart was bleeding; Susmita was indifferent. She did not love him anymore. How could he live now? He was simply unable to bear Susmita's apathy. What should he do now? She was growing more and more indifferent towards him, like all the others, and gave him nothing but suffering.

Suddenly, Susmita placed her palm on Debarchan's. Debarchan, shocked as if a strong current was flowing into his body, stammered, "Why does your hand feel so cold, Susmita?"

Susmita shot back, "Why does your hand feel like steel, Debarchan?"

Debarchan's body stiffened. He took Susmita's icy hands into his and held them silently. He knew they had exhausted what they had to say; they ran short of words now, to communicate, to respond. Henceforth, they would only repeat the same words to each other. There was no alternative. They had nothing to give to each other anymore.

It was Susmita who broke the lingering silence. "What is it that we call happiness, Debarchan?"

Debarchan was speechless. Susmita went further. "What are you for me, Debarchan, my happiness or my suffering?"

It was strange something similar was troubling Debarchan and he was about to ask Susmita a similar question. But who knows, if his answer had crossed Susmita's, what then? He chose not to speak anymore. Perhaps Susmita was not expecting an answer.

Life went on. Debarchan survived; Susmita survived. The rats too made their presence felt in the house. The furniture of the house was minced into bits, the files at Debarchan's office were reduced to dust. Rats steered his entire world of success. And at such moments of despair, what did Susmita offer but her demented laughter? She laughed at all his futile moves and this deflated him.

One evening, there was no more work at the office. Debarchan should have returned to his home, to its multiple miseries: the varied tyrannies of the rats, the filth, and Susmita's hysterical outbursts signalling his failures. He knew he would wear out. So he did not walk home, but instead, strolled about aimlessly until he found himself at Mr. Samantray's gate.

Mr. Samantray had gone out but Mrs. Samantray was there. The whole house was in a state of confusion. The squalid drawing room held a messy array of books, clothes, and utensils. Dust flew about everywhere. Everything was in a state of chaos. The house was filled with rats, rats who ate into the sofa-set covers and the door curtains. Books, sarees, petticoats, pants, shirts were torn into scraps -- rat-eaten scraps.

Did Mrs. Samantray have rats in her house too? Were the rats around everywhere? Had they infested the entire town?

Mrs. Samantray was there withdrawn and grief-stricken. She asked Debarchan to sit. Debarchan, settling down in a chair, remarked, "What a mess all around."

Mrs. Samantray grumbled, "Rats. What else?"

"We too have them at home," Debarchan remarked.

Rats were tearing apart every object in the house. Yet how cool did she appear to be? She was just like Susmita!

"I feel great despair," she complained.

"So do I, Mrs. Samantray," Debarchan responded.

"No one understands me."

"No one understands me either, Mrs. Samantray."

"I am so lonely."

"I am too -- very lonely."

Debarchan had found in Mrs. Samantray a kindred soul who also was experiencing great sadness like him. Who else but she could be close to him? Just see, while that day he was panic-stricken over Susmita's grief, he was now being drawn to Mrs. Samantray by her melancholy. Agonies differ with people.

Debarchan got up and sat near Mrs. Samantray. Mrs. Samantray too edged towards him. He bent over her. She put her hand on his shoulders and caressed his back. He said, "I am very sad, very dejected."

Mrs. Samantray craned her face towards Debarchan, her breath hot. She wailed, "Only you can pull me out of my melancholy, Debarchan."

Debarchan rubbed his lips against Mrs. Samantray's and thrust his tongue into her mouth. Mrs. Samantray's tongue, wet, felt Debarchan's tongue. Debarchan bit her lower lip. She unbuttoned her top. Then...

... a storm broke— a tornado. Mrs. Samantray's soft bosom offered Debarchan a wide valley. Where like a toddler who is born blind, he lost himself. A merchant ship wafted along the sea like an olive leaf. The ship on its voyage across the sea stopped at the island-of-clove. In the island-of-clove was a mesmerized Mona Lisa with pearls, rubies, and diamonds dribbling from her body; a Mona Lisa bathed in semi-slumber, her body ablaze with a starry illumination. Then, cracks from a sudden earthquake; fossils pulverized; phosphorus splinter. The wind turned into a gale as if the wind-god was celebrating a festival. The gale frightened the snake, Satan, so much it glided back into the hole. Satan went into hiding. Then the storm subsided. It was the end of summer and in came winter, abruptly. In winter, the snake hibernated; it does not stir. . .

"What happened to me? What did you do to me?" a miserable Mrs. Samantray pleaded to Debarchan.

Debarchan's lips were sealed.

She continued, "You forced me to sin. Sin, only sin is around me, Deb." Debarchan was speechless still.

"Chhi ... I hate it. Why didn't I die, before this could happen? No redemption for me I know. I won't find a place even in hell." Debarchan's face had dropped; he had not opened his mouth yet.

"Go away, please. Just go away,' Mrs. Samantray pleaded.

As he walked home, Debarchan decided, No. No more of this. No more of this meaningless living that does not lead one anywhere. Enough of this existence that guides one to ruin, yielding to the sovereignty of rats. Every husband had a lover hidden in him whom we cannot see; so also does every wife. A house exists within the four walls only if someone seeks one. Now a husband seeks a lover beyond his wife; the wife seeks a lover beyond her husband. Then a couple hunts for a house beyond their four walls.

But what does one actually acquire, anyway, in such a pursuit? What does one get in return except guilt and disappointment? Is it not better to head homewards? To return home and accept Susmita as she is? Yes, it is the best solution, the best.

Debarchan came home. Dry, gray pellets of rat feces were scattered around. Sarees reduced to rags, eaten by rats hung loose from the sofa-chairs. Books, cigarette butts, and used teacups were strewn as usual in the bedroom. Rats played with him, openly and ostentatiously. One mounted his foot.

Susmita too had retired into her own world. She was completely oblivious to Debarchan's presence. She sat by the window quietly, just looking out. She did not hasten to prepare snacks or tea for Debarchan, nor did she chat with him, not even a few tittering polite words. She kept on sitting there mutely, staring blankly at the sky, trying to figure out forms in the vacuum. . .

But Debarchan had already made up his mind. Going forward, he would yield to such circumstances. He would maintain a hold on his true self and fight against the dark days. He would at least combat the rats. He would breathe—along with Susmita, his own Susmita.

He got down to clearing the entire house. He swept away the rats and, in the process, swept up the dust from the floor; mopped up the burnt cigarette butts; and washed the teacups. He gathered the shreds of clothes and assembled the scraps of books and papers. He killed many rats with his broom. Oh, what a huge number of rats lay lifeless on the floor.

But Susmita remained aloof. She continued to stand statue-like by the window, throwing empty glances at the sky occasionally. She gaped at Debarchan's efforts but never came forward to help him with his activities or efforts.

Debarchan was trying to bring a semblance of beauty to the house again. He tugged at the sofa cover to hide the slits. The ravaged patch on the wall was veiled and the tear on the curtain was tucked out of sight. But Susmita was hardly bothered.

She did not walk up to him; did not join him in redecorating the house; did not suggest what they should do to reverse the look the house had worn of late; and to seal off the rat-holes.

Still, Debarchan did not give up. Halfway through refurbishing the house, feeling exhausted, he fell into a sleep too deep for dreams and woke up in darkness. What darkness, man! It was almost about midnight. Debarchan saw Susmita beside him like a corpse. Was it very late at night? How come Susmita did not wake him for supper? How could she sleep like that?

This time Debarchan did not lose his temper. He had vowed he would mould himself uniquely; live up to Susmita's expectations.

Debarchan felt he would draw Susmita to his lap and kiss her and whisper into her ear: "Let's change, Susmita. Let's change into unique human beings."

Debarchan was trying to reach out for Susmita. But how amazing. He could not stretch his hands. Strange, he could not even stir, though his limbs loosened and began to unfasten from their sockets. Only his trunk was left. It was rolling like the mythical Kabandha.

And precisely at that moment, the worst happened. A

rumbling sound from somewhere suddenly filtered into Debarchan's ears. Where was it coming from? Was it from the ceiling? From near his head? From under the cot? Was it from outside or was it coming from within the house?

Thinking thus, Debarchan looked at his own chest. God! A rat was on his chest. It had settled there and was digging into his ribs. The rat was carving a hole into Debarchan's heart.

Debarchan panicked and wanted to raise his hand in order to smack the creature off him. But his arm was just hanging loose from the joint and could not move. He was overcome by helplessness, his vision blurred with tears flooding from his eyes. He wanted to scream for Susmita and tell her about the rat that was going to end his life. But nothing escaped his lips -- nothing. Alas! Debarchan was paralyzed. His lips were shut. His limbs had become immobile. What would he do now?

And see, what a coincidence Susmita had to wake from her sleep just now, at this wretched hour. She had to peep and spot the rat pulling him to pieces. And as if that was not enough, she had to let loose her incessant bursts of laughter.

What uproarious laughter. Susmita's sides were splitting ha-ha, ho-ho ... Susmita was breaking into cackles, her stomach crumpled into a lump in her fist. Large salty beads ran out of her nostrils. The snickers, however, were ceaseless.

Susmita was going crazy with laughter. "What fun," she interjected occasionally. "It is perforating your ribs, man. It is penetrating your heart. The rat is feasting on your heart!"

Susmita's frenzied giggles spread all over and the rat settled comfortably on Debarchan's spread out trunk, drilling into his breast.

A SITA IN THE ASHOK FOREST

"A dying colliery, people say. No, more like the Ashok Forest," said Pratima. "Remember the Ashok Forest? That was where poor Sita was imprisoned."

Pratima was a nurse on a basic salary of 630 rupees a month to which was added the dearness allowance, the variable dearness allowance and the incentive bonus of ten percent. Plenty, in a manner of speaking. So, what ailed the poor girl? What was the cause of her sorrow? Why did she wallow in self-pity? Why did she think of herself as a Sita in the Ashok Forest?

Pratima's Soliloquy

My life is empty of all joy and happiness, its pristine whiteness sullied by globs of dirt. Of course, nothing better could be expected in this God-forsaken colliery. Here, people spend as much or maybe more than what they earn -- and they earn handsome amounts, mind you, compared to others -- and just a week or so after pay day, they head for the Afghan moneylenders. None makes a serious attempt to improve their quality of life.

Did I ever imagine I'd get stranded in a hole like this? It's an awful place; a barren patch. Nothing will ever blossom here and I'm trapped in a silent house with nothing but memories to go over and over again.

The house, my house: three rooms, an inner courtyard, a kitchen, a storeroom, and a toilet. What do I need so much space for? I have nothing to fill its void with. Sometimes I wish that the house was chock full of bric-a-brac and that I had a man, someone after my heart of course, and maybe a little child. I lie in bed and dream and my eyes well up with tears.

I live alone so all I really need is just one room. For a long time after I moved in here, I never opened the windows of the rooms I didn't use them until I found white ants having a merry go at the woodwork. The curtains too had been eaten. Since then, I've made it a point to open the windows every morning and dust them; check the curtains and air them. But that's about all, the rest of the day the windows stay shut.

The place my house is located is called Number Eight by the locals, named after the pit which was once operational here. It had to be closed down after water began to ooze out of its depths. Until then, the place hummed with activity and bustled with people. Some people thought the colliery was a blessed heaven but after the mine was closed, just about anyone and everyone who could pull strings with the administration moved on to better places. Those, like me who couldn't, stayed behind.

I have very little contact with my neighbors. There's one Murthy - a Telegu fellow and a bachelor. I don't even know his full name; haven't spoken a word with him ever. Then there's a certain Singh. He has a big, thick moustache and came across as anti-social. Whenever we run into each other, he asks, "How are you, Sister - all right?" His accent betrays his Bihari origin. I don't know his full name either but he lives alone too. Then there are a few others I know only by sight. Some say hello; some flash a smile; and some inquire if I am doing fine.

When I first arrived here, a horde of women from the colony descended on me in a gesture of good neighborliness. They asked about my home, parents, marital status, the cost of my sarees, and praised their husbands. Only later did I realize the real purpose of their visit: acquaintance with a nurse might come in handy someday. A few, of course, came out of sheer curiosity. Anyway, the neighborly visits soon dwindled and then stopped altogether. Of the whole lot, I can count on my fingers the ones I remember: Mrs. Jadav, Mrs. Sinha, Mrs. Srivastava, Miss Mohanty. The rest I've forgotten.

Hospital duty is eight hours. The doctor usually reports late, so there's plenty of free time; the actual grind never exceeds five or five-and-a-half hours. The rest of the time you sit, chat and laugh. And then you go home to your little prison, cook, tidy up, wash clothes, browse through much-subbed novels, fiddle with the transistor radio. Anything, just any damn thing to kill time. But is it easy to kill time? The clock stops, time dilates. Like a midnight train plagued by constant chain-pulling; despite blowing whistle after whistle, it hardly chugs ahead. Wistfully, I look forward to the morning station. When will the train reach there? I turn, I toss, I sit up on my bed; I fiddle with the radio, I move the pointer from one dead centre to another. The room I'm imprisoned in expands, looms ever larger; the blast of emptiness rings out.

That's my life in a nutshell in the Ashok Forest. I can't get along with my neighbors; I don't even try. In the evenings, when smoke curls up from the coal ovens all around my house, I get out of breath. And that's when I feel what a big blob of dirt this colliery life is and how utterly devoid of freshness life is in the Ashok Forest.

The Ashok Forest -- it's got a romantic ring to it, hasn't it? It feels so good to imagine yourself as a wilting Sita. But where's Ram? Where's the rescuer in my life? I entered the Ashok Forest long before I could pick out a Ram. I could have, though. There were many men hovering around me, but nothing ever worked out. Nothing came very close to anything serious. No one stopped by long enough to contemplate marriage.

In the last year of school, there was this friend of mine, Vishnupriya, whose elder brother caught hold of me one evening and insisted in the presence of others on feeding me a handful of rice puffs. I felt shy, but I did open my mouth and his moist fingers brushed across my lips. The sensation stayed fresh for days and anytime I wanted to I could feel his moist fingers on my lips, God knows, it fed many of my dreams. It also inspired the first, and also the last, story I ever wrote.

It started fading when I finished school and went to Cuttack to train as a nurse. And there, Mannadidi, one of the senior girls, warned me: beware of the roving eyes in the medical campus. Show the slightest bit of interest and they will gobble you up alive. Don't ever let your guard down.

But did I heed her words of caution? Maybe no one got wind of it. Maybe the only three people involved in the whole thing were God, Amit and myself. But I did steal into the Female Ward one night, eluding the watchful eyes of the sisters and attendant. I thought I'd just speak a few words with Amit, who was on duty there. But I let him lead me to the deserted post office behind the pharmacology lab and make love to me. The pleasure was as great as the accompanying pain and I came back to the hostel crushed under guilt and had to invent a lie that I had been to see a distant aunt in the Female Ward. That night, I could hardly sleep, gripped by fear and fathomless joy. Luckily, it was my safe period.

Shortly afterwards, Amit drifted away. Men continued to

seek me out but I played hard to get. Amit's betrayal drove home the lesson: men were pariahs to be kept at a distance; bring them a little closer and you started to melt like wax yourself. The heat they (the men) give off, Hungry eyes followed me everywhere but then the training came to an end and I landed this job through the employment exchange. And here, ever since I came, life has been awful: lonely, cocooned in a dense fog of despair. So much for my life in the Ashok Forest.

In Front of Pratima's House

Here came Pratima wrapped in a white saree. Tired, weary, her hair disheveled and flying in the breeze. Plastic chapels. Long, chipping fingernails, remnants of cheap nail polish on them. The coat no. 1 talcum powder coming off her face in patches; rivulets of sweat; the kola fading from the rims of her eyes; cheap jewelry dangling from her ears; a bare neck; two glass bangles on her right wrist and a watch on the left -- the watch had stopped ages ago. Pratima was in limbo: no past, no present, no future. Everything was the same to her. Her eyes seem drowned in a bottomless pool of fatigue. Her white cap dangled limply from her left hand. In her right hand, she held a purse and a small ladies' handkerchief with which she wiped the grime off her face from time to time.

Pratima stopped in front of her house. She opened her purse, took out a bunch of keys and chose one, leaned forward on her toes, and grasping her cap and purse between her teeth, inserted the key into the lock and turned it. She pulled down the latch and pushed open the door.

Pratima's Sitting Room

When the clear creaks opened, Pratima put one foot inside. Outside, it was getting dark. The light switch behind the door was on the left. She turned, stretched her right hand, groped around awhile and then flicked the switch on. The room was flooded with light. She closed the door and stood for a moment looking down around her feet. The postman always pushed any mail under the door.

Today, there were no letters but a piece of paper instead. Pratima was a little surprised. She still had her cap in her left hand and her purse in her right. Transferring her purse to her left, she juggled both and stooped down to pick up the paper.

It was neatly folded in four and seemed to have been pulled out from a lined notebook. The handwriting had no great shakes and a couple of spelling errors jumped out at her at a casual glance. Oh my, it's a letter, a letter that hadn't come in the mail. Somebody had slipped it under the door.

She began to read. On the top is a regular epigraph:

'Some love one, some love two

I love one, that is you.'

And below that:

'Queen of my heart!'

She crumpled it into a ball and held it tightly. She knew what it was. Letters like this she had received in piles during her training. Her heart began to beat faster and faster. Her mouth went dry.

Pratima's Bedroom

Curtains in the windows shut out the outside. There was a single mattress on a string cot; an ugly old tin trunk in a corner squatting on bricks; a cheap leather suitcase on top of the trunk; an attaché case on top of the suitcase, wrapped in a cover made out of old clothes. On a shelf, there was a small tin of talcum powder; a bottle of face cream; a bottle of shampoo; a bottle of nail polish; a few bangles in a cardboard box; a picture album. The empty box of a wall clock was on another shelf. There were a few much-thumbed-through, dog-eared novels, some by Bibhuti Patnaik, all covered in yellowing newsprint with Pratima's name written in bold letters on top.

A large mirror on the eight by eight wall. A wooden clothes rack stood in a corner with a few clean neatly folded sarees hanging from it with the straps of the brassieres tucked underneath the sarees peeping out. Folded blouses and petticoats. A hand-knitted cardigan sweater. All a picture of neatness. Everything was in order. An overpowering feminine smell and presence enveloped the room.

Pratima walked into her bedroom. She did not bother to change her clothes. She switched on the light and the fan. Depositing her cap, purse and keys on the top shelf, she walked to the bed and sat down, leaning against the wall. She slowly loosened her fist and the ball of crumpled paper dropped on to the bed. She uncrumpled it and smoothed it across her thigh, reading it again.

A Love Letter for Pratima
'Some love one, some love two
I love one, that is you.
Queen of my heart!'
The day I first saw you I don't know why but I fell in love with you. Your image constantly haunts me. I see you everywhere -- in my dreams too.

Dear Sister, why do you laugh and chat so much with those two good-far-nothing pharmacists at the hospital? One of them, the one called Das, is one hell of son of a bitch. He receives letters from any number of girls. I found this out from the post office. No fewer than eight to ten letters a day. Who do you think wrote to him if not girls? And that other fellow, that Khuntia, well, he had an affair with Sister Hira; the whole colliery knew about it. Imagine how I felt the other day when I saw you sitting on the same bench as those two characters, chatting away about nothing in particular. Dear one, they are out to trap you. Beware!

That doctor chap is no good either. Do you know he doesn't get along with his wife? Well, he too has his eyes on you. Beware!

My Queen, don't be cross with me for coming out with all this. My only desire is your safety and well-being. I am pining for you like a chakor bird does for his mate. I lost my heart to you at the first glance, remember. I dream of you, oh so many dreams - but alas, when the dream's over and I awaken, I find myself painfully alone in my bed.

Flower of my love, I want to tie the knot with you. Are you willing? Can you give up everything for my sake? Will you be mine? If you are willing, then place a brick in front of your house when you go to hospital tomorrow morning. That will be the sign, and in my next letter I will divulge my name and address. Suffice it to say we have met each other not once but several times. You have given me injections no fewer than five times. Looking forward to your consent.

Tea for milk, milk for tea
I for you, you for me
Thirsting for your love,

Your unknown friend.

Pratima's Reaction

Who sent this outrageous letter, who? How many such stupid love letters have I received so far? This one, of course, had come after a long, long time. The last one I received was in Cuttack, which I've left behind together with my void life. It seemed another life now. Who in this dead colliery ...?

Who could it be? The letter reads like a young greenhorn's, like a boy of sixteen or seventeen. Oh mother mine, was he younger than me? Look at the handwriting and the spelling errors. And a marriage proposal to boot in the very first love letter? I don't even know this fellow from Adam! Look at his lurid style: Queen of my heart, flower of my love. What nonsense! Who does he think he's writing to? A high school girl? How dare he propose marriage? If he has courage, why doesn't he come forward and introduce himself first? The marriage proposal can wait. Why has he taken to writing letters? Am I to believe I got a letter from a young boy I don't even know? Everyone will think I must have led him down the garden path.

What if he comes over now? Suppose he comes and knocks

and when I open the door . . . suppose he simply barges in and . . . he. . . Oh mother mine, I'm all alone. The colony is so deserted that no help would turn up even if I were to scream. What if he turns out to be a regular hoodlum? What will I do then, what?

Who can it be? Not Murthy, oh no; it can't be him. Not Singh either by a long stretch. Neither of them knows Oriya. And the fellow says I have given him injections. Now who are the young boys who have regularly been to the hospital? Oh dammit, I can't remember a single face. How can a nurse remember the faces of all the people she's given injections to?

Can it be Das? Or Khuntia? One or the other or both together might have done it for the heck of it. Who knows? You can't trust men. What will I do if they decide to barge into my house at night? Oh God! I received so many of these damned letters in medical college but I was never so scared. What's the matter with me? Why am I so nervous? Is it because I live alone, because there's no one around to come to my rescue? And how would I protect myself? Sister Kanaka, that irrepressible tomboy of a trainee nurse who once hit a house surgeon for a misdemeanor and sang a bawdy song acting as a professor, what could she do if two drunken louts from Mangalabag pinned her down to the floor in the NET ward? If the ward attendants hadn't responded to her frantic screams, she would have been raped. But how can I ward off an attack if and when it comes?

Pratima in the Bedroom

Pratima was in bed lying on her stomach with her legs bent and raised and shaking spasmodically. Her face was buried deep in the pillow.

She raised herself on her elbows and opened her eyes. She fished out the letter from under the pillow and read: 'I am pining for you like a chakor bird does for his mate. I lost my heart to you at the first glance, remember. I dream of you, oh so many dreams - but alas, when the dream's over and I awaken, I find myself painfully alone in my bed.'

She folded it. Her uniform crushed, her feet dirty, her hair tousled; she sat like a log. She made no effort to prepare tea or do nothing to start dinner. It was seven o'clock already. She did not look at the radio, did not fiddle with it to tune in Radio Ceylon.

Her fingers closed around the letter and her fist tightened into a knot again. Her head drooped and her face burrowed into the pillow. She raised her legs and rocked them. Suddenly she got up and turned the whirring fan to a faster speed. She stood in the middle of the room, but only for a moment. Then she went back to the cot and slumped down onto the bed again. Her fist opened. She smoothed the letter and read on: 'Flower of my love, I want to tie the knot with you. Are you willing? Can you give up everything for my sake? Will you be mine?'

She crumpled the letter. A smile spread over her face, bringing a little color into it. She got up and walked to the shelf, emptied the cardboard box containing the bangles, placed the letter at the bottom and put back the bangles and then the box. She looked at herself in the tiny hand mirror, running her fingers through her untidy hair. Like a Sita in the Ashok Forest, she whispers to herself. Yeah.

Why does she repeat it to herself? Why does she repeat it and then burst out laughing bitterly?

Epilogue

The next morning as she started for the hospital, Pratima stopped by her door, her legs heavy and ready to send down roots. She remembered the letter, looked around and saw a broken piece of brick lying nearby. She started. She then picked the brick up and threw it as far away as she could. She surveyed the surroundings carefully again. No more bricks.

●●

In the hospital, she could not take her mind off the letter, no matter how hard she tried. She viewed everyone she met with suspicion - it could be anyone, just anyone. Who knew? But no one seemed likely, even remotely.

It then occurred to her the broken piece of brick she saw in front of her house might have been left by a child who came to play. She need not have panicked.

When she went back to her house at noon, there was no brick, broken or whole, in sight. She pushed open the door of the house and looked down at the floor. Nothing there.

At three o'clock, she returned to hospital and until six, thought of nothing but the letter. And then it was time to go home.

When she opened her door in the evening, she searched the floor again. Somewhere in the recesses of her heart she had a lurking hope there would be another letter. No matter how much she would have loved to pretend the contrary, she longed for a letter which would have felt like the gentle brushing of moist fingers across her lips. But the floor was bare.

Days passed, one after another after another. Pratima went to work, returned home, stared at the floor, hoped for a message scribbled in royal blue ink on lined paper from a notebook. She never got one.

Months passed. Pratima continued to take care of her hair, cook her meals, wash her clothes, keep her rooms spanking clean, changed her bedsheets frequently, did her duties at the hospital quite diligently. Her time passed - mornings, afternoons, evenings. Night after night, she lay on the bed with the transistor radio on her breast and listlessly moved the knob from one end to the other, not tuning to any station in particular. She strained her ears to pick out the sounds of the dark: the chirping of crickets, distant drumbeats, the whirring of the fan, the commotion at the neighbor's. A life lived alone is a life wasted, she often whispered to herself. It was a life of sorrow, like the life of a Sita in the Ashok Forest. A life of lingering pain. She would lie wide awake late into the night, her breath hot and ragged. Sometimes she would get up and walk to the shelf, take down the cardboard box and retrieve the letter from underneath the bangles. A piece of paper torn from a lined notebook, a message scribbled in royal blue ink. 'Flower of my love, I want to tie the knot with you. Are you willing? Can you give up everything for my sake? Will you be mine?' She would read it slowly, with a strange sensation of someone moving his moist fingers across her lips. Shaken to her innermost core, she would close her eyes and whisper: Oh, you little coward, why didn't you ever write again?

■

THE GOLDEN FISH

It was dusk by the time we reached Chandipur. A sudden cloudburst had barred our way. On the wayside was stretched out the weekly village market. For a distance, the road heading towards the Missile Testing Centre pulled us magically. No sooner did Pupun free himself from the hypnotic lure than he was stopped by a herd of deer.

At the shore, it seemed as if the sea had turned its back in a sulking mood. Archana was, of course, not thrilled. There was opulence in the sea at Puri. Solemnity at Gopalpur and fearful solitude at Konarka's Chandrabhaga. The sea at Chandipur was different from all these, a rustic beauty in a fashion show you might say!

••

Beneath our feet, there were terrified crabs, scurrying for their lives, frantically diving into the sand for cover. This had startled Pupun. Was the crab a vegetarian or a meat eater? Pupun, who got 98 percent marks in the examination of class three and secured third position, did not quite know the answer. Do I have the answer? There were so many mysteries I do not know: man's birth and death, the many universes like our own. Clearly there was a lot I knew nothing about!

●●

Archana called out: "Pupun, let's go and touch the waves!"

"Yes, go and hug them!" urged the tourists. Soon the sea was going to recede two or three kilometers. Scared, Pupun said in a desperate act of self-assurance: "There is no crab here!"

"It will do you no harm Pupun!" I assured him.

"Crabs eat meat. It's a maneater! After all, man dies by the sting of a scorpion!"

"Well, crab and scorpion are not one and the same, you know! The crab certainly does not eat men."

"Of course, it does!"

"Take my word Pupun! My experience of forty long years," I said, "Believe me, the crab does not eat men!"

Pupun's eyes showed signs of disbelief. The shore at Chandipur was gradually receding. Archana called out, "Come on Pupun. Come and touch the waves!"

●●

"Why are you so scared, my son? How can you secure life from fire, water, air, accidents and death? Listen, life can never be transient! Fire cannot burn it, water cannot drown it, and air cannot blow it! Only in the hand of an assassin do we finally die! Offer your salutation to him, not to the pyre, nor water, nor air! Roll life like a ball! Let it roll on the hard soil, dry grass, thorn and the rocks! And then, you will see that you have gone ahead my boy! Or else, you will find yourself forever standing still!"

●●

Pupun did not proceed further. He could not believe we

had taken up fear as the dress of custom. He could not remove that dress. And yet, his whole life would be spent in the stifling heat.

I screamed, "Go Pupun, go! Go to the sea!" Pupun did not move. He released his defiant hand from my trusting first. I shook in anger. Landing a big blow on his back, I yelled, "Go to the sea you little coward!"

Hearing my scream, two tourists turned back. The girl singing Rabindra Sangeet abruptly stopped. The sea got scared and receded a few steps. Archana moved forward and taking Pupun in her lap, remonstrated, "Just, what do you think you are doing? If you insult the child before everyone, don't you think he will develop a complex?"

••

Pupun's birth had completely changed my world. Stepping out of the operation theater of the nursing home, the nurse had let me hold the newborn baby. With him snuggled between my two palms, I had entered into a strange new world that recognized no distinction between obscenity and propriety. Only nudity made for beauty here. Until yesterday, the woman who concealed her motherhood in public before me lay an aged world. Holding the cherubic hands, I had stepped into the world that day, precisely at 10:20 a.m. To be sure, I have always been a contented and successful man. There was no shame of South Africa in me! No problem of general election! Nobel Prize, Jnanpith or Arjuna Award! There was no 21st Century, radio activity, future of man, communal riots, fascist politics, extremism, and price rises or dearness allowance. Absolutely nothing! – Only Archana for myself and the four walls around us!

And inside? Well, sofa, TV, dining table, glass almirah, carpet, cooler for the heat of summer and room heater and geyser for the cold season. Also, there was mixie, hot pack, Banarasi saree, coat, suit, expensive quartz watches, a scooter – and Archana's growing waist line.

At that moment, Pupun was our only achievement. Three

years after our marriage, every one near and far, the in-laws as well, as well our own people – meaning the whole society – had become obsessed with a single thought: why was there no Pupun in our life! As it was, Archana had irregular periods. Before her sanguine encounter every time, she used to dream that Pupun had come into her womb. And yet, there had been no sign of Pupun, only a bloody coldness!

I had little shame or guilt as to why there was no Pupun in our life, much as Archana forever agonized about it. We had a good bungalow and scooter. There was jewelry in the bank's locker. And we had status and social prestige. Only, there was no Pupun! That did not seem to matter, at any rate to me! However, Archana's opinion was just the opposite, that in every one's life there had to be a Pupun! Everyone was capable of creating a Pupun! Only I was not! This was the burden of Archana's sorrow and complaint.

After Pupun's arrival, our roles were reversed. The one who had prayed for Pupun kneeling down at the altar of 33 crore temples, bathing in the tank of Marich, she had lost all desires! Her sleep never got disturbed at night and she nearly forgot the date of her Polio injection. Shaking the box of baby food at night, she would remark, "Goodness, the baby food is over!" When Pupun had loose movements, she would say, "None of them is necessary! Only a glass of sherbet with a pinch of salt and sugar will do the trick!"

●●

A handful of Bengali tourists loitering on the beach turned and looked at us. Taking the injured self of Pupun on her lap, Archana admonished me: "You should never insult a child before others, it will only aggravate his complex." And then she said to Pupun, "Come Baba, come my dear! The crab is not going to harm you!"

Shaking off his mother's hand, Pupun ran on and looked back. Eyes laden with anguish, he said: "All right, I shall tell my friends that my father is a demon who flings me into the sea!" Saying this, he fled on the beach.

Archana called him back: "Pupun darling, come and leave your shoes behind!" But Pupun was in no mood to comply.

●●

Holding the hand of Pupun, I had learnt how to walk. When Pupun had fallen down as a toddler, it was I who had cried the most despite his utter helplessness. I had suffered his constipation! And it was his hunger that forever fueled the fire in my stomach! Pupun's cry had always upset our world.

Once when Pupun was one-and-a-half years old, he had cried out in the middle of the night. What could possibly be meant by the adventure of an infant? It was neither a war cry, a charter of demands, nor a slogan! "What is it Pupun? Would you like some water?" Pupun pushed away the glass of water with his hand. "Want a comb? Or a ball? Here, take this box or read the newspaper! A, B, C, D! One, two, three, four! Want to remove powder from the box from the lower shelf of the dressing table? Want to pull out the broken clock from the drawer? Hairpin or imitation jewelry? All right! Now take this doll or that bear, tiger, cat or zebra. Or else, take the elephant that resembles a bear! Or the dog that resembles a jackal!"

Disinclined, Pupun pushed away everything. Suddenly, my happy and successful household had crumbled miserably into poverty. I had everything and yet had nothing! For Pupun, that was my ultimate failure and disgrace! The beach at Chandipur has no chai wallah. None to sell "moori" or shells! And there was no cameraman either! A group of Bengalis were busy singing Rabindra Sangeet. In the sky was the bright orb of the moon! The sea had receded to a distance. Only its muffled roar was heard now. The scooter lay in the growing darkness. Shall we go and look for the scooter? Dash it! The light of the Panthanivas was running in the moonlight! Was it possible to have a cup of tea? What a pity! Maybe we could go down to Balamagardi. By the way, the house of John Beams was still preserved there! We could even see how the Budhabalanga River joined the sea. Goodness gracious! Such a long distance from a cup of tea! Pupun dear, do not be mad at us! Here, have some "mixture." See, the road is dangerously dark, interspersed with pits! It's a new place after all!

●●

Pupun's first day in school was a real experience. You should have seen Archana cry after seeing Pupun onto the bus. The house appeared utterly empty. With her head on my shoulder Archana sobbed as though she had placed Pupun on the funeral pyre! A few days earlier, I was totally lost in Pupun's dream world of a new uniform, tiffin box, and water bottle. For the first time, Pupun could sense what it meant to have his own possessions: school box, note books, pencil, eraser, tiffin box, and water bottle. My sofa, color TV, air cooler, scooter, mixie, and cooking gas, all appeared distinctly trival before Pupun's gleaming new estate. Equally worthless was Archana's jewelry. We returned to the nursery rhymes. Like "Jack and Jill," we climbed up the hill to fetch water and tumbled down one after the other!

As for Pupun, he used to return like a battle tested veteran with dog-eared torn books, shoes grimed with cow-dung, matched with dirty shirt and pants. At times, the casualties included lost buttons and money, forcing poor Archana and me to join the battle. We could always sense his helplessness, like Abhimanyu, of facing single-handed, seven warriors.

"Why didn't you beat the daylight out of the chap that hit you? You should have pulled out his hair! Should have jabbed his eye with pencil or else bitten him! What were your teachers doing? Must have been busy, as usual, in their gossip sessions! Or else surely knitting their sweaters! Couldn't you tell them?

●●

Leaving the beach behind, we went looking for tea inside the village. When we returned, there was the sea still at a distance. Everywhere, there was a pallid moon. The beach floor shone with a silvery light! We sat on a broken wall, packet snacks in Archana's hands "Here, Pupun, help yourself!" I said. Pupun, of course, had no interest. No crabs were visible in the darkness. The light from the Panthanivas lent a sepulchral glow. Suddenly, a jeep drove down the beach.

Shall we go to the waves? Archana asked.

"Yes, let us!" Pupun shouted aloud, his voice making the girl singing Rabindra Sangeet turn back.

●●

Pupun's Convert School vocabulary had always been a matter of enigma for me and Archana. There were many words we simply could not grasp and some, we could not imagine using in our conversation. These words were outside his nursery rhymes and books; perfectly abusive and unprintable expressions. Pupun, the war veteran's account, never failed to amaze and worry us. His vengeful self, always spawned nails and teeth, his unseen eyes, cruel laughter, and his invisible face sported pride. Once again, we returned to our study of moral science. Once again, we spoke parrot-like, "Always speak the truth Pupun. Get up early in the morning. See what a wonderful day God has created. Pupun, come and eat what ma has served you. Read what Baba has given you. Go and play Pupun. Never quarrel with anyone. Return good for evil. Return kiss for abuse. And if slapped on one cheek, show the other."

●●

There was now water beneath one's feet and yet they did not get wet. Only one sensed the feel of wet, sandy, and muddy earth. Everywhere on the beach of Chandipur was spread out a layer of silvery moonlight. Archana's emotional utterance, "Never have I seen such a sea in my life," and my state of meditative absentmindedness had articulated earlier, "I was not impressed by the first sight of Chandipur!," from all these Pupun walks away in a spirit of detachment.

Throwing a glance at him. Archana said, "You know, Pupun's virtue is that he has scrupulously followed our model of upbringing. But tell me, how exactly have we wished him to grow up? Do we really know what it means to be a good man?"

Pupun's mind no longer had the fear of crab. Walking ahead,

he asked, "Mummy, is there a golden fish in the sea?" Pupun's life was sandwiched between Archana's college, her computer class, my office, and our empty house. When Pupun woke up, Archana had gone to her class. And when Pupun returned from school, Archana was at her college and I was in my office. Pupun waited for the maidservant. It was a persistent worry! Suppose the maid was absent? Suppose there was a big lock on the door upon his return?

"Why do you worry darling?" I would say. "Are we not there to think of you? If the maidservant was absent, then we would be there. Mummy or I would certainly take leave and stay back."

"I feel scared Baba. I am still scared." Pupun would reply.

"Why do you fear, my dear? Am I not there? I would answer reassuringly.

●●

Get up at five in the morning. Be in your mad rush with Pupun in mind. Ring up from the office. Find out if Pupun had returned. Had Archana returned? Ring up the garage of the school bus. Is the school bus okay? Is the driver on duty or is he on leave? Ring up Archana's college. Find out if she had her staff council meeting. In the evening, on the way back, collect Pupun from the playground and make him do his homework.

With all this, one was naturally unhinged. At the time, Pupun sought out his own destiny, devoid of parental contact and announced, "Give me the key Ma when you're in your computer class. I shall keep sitting in the drawing room and ring up Baba in case I feel scared!" Only at such times did Archana notice that Pupun was no keener to play or mix with anyone. He watched other children at play from a distance. Helpless, he sat absentminded at the study table, forgetting his addition, subtraction, division and multiplication exercises. And when he did attend to his studies, he got arrogant and defiant.

●●

"Mummy, how does a golden fish look?" Pupun asked as he walked ahead on the beach.

Far away, there was the roar of the waves. And behind, there was the dim light of the Panthanivas. Further off were visible the flickering lights of the Missile Center's colony. Around us, there was the pale silver of the beach. In the sky, there was the moon and clouds. Beneath our feet, there was the muddy earth. Watch out, there could be quicksand somewhere. Every step appeared uncertain. "Baba Pupun, watch carefully. Come and hold our hands!"

The sea was far away. Only its roar could now be heard. Those who sang Rabindra Sangeet on the beach of Chandipur, -- Bengali tourists – they were no longer visible. At a distance, the lights of the Panthanivas were twinkling. What was right ahead? Was it a rock? Where was so much fog coming from? Could it be fog or some smoke from the sea? Or are we in the middle of the sea?"

"Mummy, what does the golden fish eat?" Pupun questioned.

Our hearts beat fast. There was no one in sight. What we called the beach was no longer visible. Had we reached the middle of the sea? Was some giant sea monster going to emerge from the deep? Will we get dragged into the depths by some undercurrent? Can't we have the glimpse of the waves or will our feet slip in?

"Mummy, what is the color of the golden fish?" Pupun pressed on.

From somewhere, there came the sound of a roar. The black rock appeared to be rearing its head. Everywhere there was the silver sea. It was there and yet it wasn't there, forever elusive. We seemed to be on our Great Journey on the waters of the still and immobile ocean. Archana gripped my hand in fear. "Let us not go any further," she said. "I am getting scared. Baba Pupun, please come back."

"Do not go any further Pupun!" I cautioned. "There could be a quicksand somewhere. There is no one around! So quiet and yet so fearful, this Nature! Come back dear! Let us get back to the beach of Chandipur! Back to the middle of the village, to the town of Balasore! Return to our town, to our house, our bed and to our secure quilt!"

Pupun kept running ahead and we were frozen by fear. Not a soul in sight. Only the sea, the moon, the sky, and the clouds. Death could be lurking somewhere. "Pupun darling, our creation, come back dear and hold our hand. Let us get back to the beach!"

●●

Pupun went scampering. Standing on the jade black rock, he exclaimed: "Look mummy, look. I have become a golden fish!" From behind the rocks, like some giant fearful demon, the sea leapt with its huge monstrous waves. We shook in fear by its turbulence and thunderous roar.

"Is the tide coming once again? Come on Pupun. We must save our dreams and our life"

A giant breaker came and dashed against the rock. Water climbed from our feet up to the knee and receded. With my hand as a grip for support, Archana cried out, "Pupun."

With the noise of the sea, the cry no longer reached me.

■